THE OTHER HAND CLAPPING

MARCO VASSI

POLO BOOKS

KNIGHTSBRIDGE PUBLISHING COMPANY
NEW YORK

This paperback edition of *The Other Hand Clapping* first
published in 1991 by Knightsbridge Publishing Company

Originally published by the Permanent Press in 1987

Published in the United States by
Knightsbridge Publishing Company
255 East 49th Street
New York, New York 10017

ISBN 1-56129-046-7

10 9 8 7 6 5 4 3 2 1
First Edition

"While the wooden man is singing,
The stone maiden starts to dance.
This cannot be reached by our consciousness.
Have you given any thought to this?"
                    from the *Bao-Jing San Mei*

— 1 —

The morning sun glittered on the bathroom tiles. Larry squinted against the glare and drew the gleaming straightedge razor across his scalp, removing the last trace of foam. His skin shone.

A bald head had nothing at all to do with the meaning of zen. Larry understood that. Yet, he found the effect pleasing. At first it had been ghastly, the skin that had never been exposed to air emerging grey and scaly. Now, after a year and a half, the flesh was the same shade as that of his face and felt silky to the touch.

The resistance he'd received from his wife, his friends, and his own conditioning almost overcame his resolution to sport the classical style, but the first Spring day raindrops splashed on his skull he was filled with such innocent sensuality that no mere social disapproval could compete.

Through the open window nature throbbed. Tall, silent, aspiring trees in the first flush of new leaves, birds on their flights of food and fancy, insects buzzing past, a sky of adamantine blue, and a scattering of slim clouds like underlinings in the void. It was impossible not to believe that all creation was alive on such a day, that each atom did not hum with consciousness. Green and blue and brown. Rhythms of a million sentient things. Unreflected awareness.

Larry washed his face and scalp and towelled himself dry. He had already been up for more than two hours, having risen before dawn, as he did every day, to begin the ritual of sitting, settling cross-legged on his round black pillow, his spine straight, eyes lidded, to watch the movement of his breath and the shuttling of his thoughts, until his brain and body grew quiet and a different quality of perception insinuated itself. He now sat for six hours a day in eight sessions of forty-five minutes each. The sitting was interspersed with a slow walking exercise, both a complement to and a relief from the utter immobility. The other waking hours were spent in the routines of daily life, which included the singular relationship he now had with Eleanor.

He and Eleanor had been married for four years when Larry first began to take the study of zen seriously, and in the two years since then something like a war had begun inside him, a series of battles that ultimately came to threaten the marriage itself. By the time he had shaved his head he had attended three *sesshins*, seven-day intensives in which no one spoke and everyone sat for from twelve to fourteen hours a day. Those experiences had given him a taste of the kind of power to be found in such awesome concentration and, although he tried not to, he couldn't help comparing it with what he got from his marriage.

Larry examined his face in the mirror. "I know that I know," he thought, "My highest attainment and the greatest obstacle to enlightenment." He was discovering that zen was like a strong poison used to cure a virulent disease. Zen, the most austere of concepts, was the sword with which one had to cut through the web of conceptualization altogether, and the final trap was to be mired in zen itself.

He was at that stage of involvement called "the great doubt," a psychological impasse which one school of zen insists must be raised in order to be transcended. In his case it took the form of a painful realization that he could no longer see anything directly, and he wondered if he ever had. The practice of zen often produced nothing but a deepening of his confusion, and it dawned on him that all the yogic discipline and all the teachings of the masters was little more than a distraction and consolation for the fact that he, and perhaps everyone, had lost his primal simplicity.

He looked at the man in the mirror and for an instant superimposed the image of his conventional life on that of the peculiar person who stared back at him. He was thirty-seven years old, the owner of a bookstore in Manhattan, and married to an excessively beautiful and vibrantly intelligent woman who loved him to the point of exasperation. Their marriage was based on the vision they'd shared when they met, one of classical romance in which the very union was to provide all the spiritual and aesthetic context they'd ever need. They lived in a large apartment on Central Park West and had more than enough friends and acquaintances. All they lacked to complete the picture of success was a child.

That was Eleanor's decision. She wanted a career as an actress and wouldn't consider having a baby until she'd either made some major breakthrough or become convinced that it was futile to pursue it further. She'd majored in drama at Sarah Lawrence, been praised highly by her teachers, and gone to New York to take the theatre by storm. After a few years, however, she found herself stalled in the wings and was practical enough to understand that it would be pointless to flutter like an excited moth indefinitely against the cold lights of the Great White Way. She decided to descend into the underground, in the mid 60s a network of small studios, cafe theatres, and off-off-Broadway productions. There she found a lively spirit of experimentation. She studied and worked and waitressed and had affairs and lived out the metatheatre which pervaded the structure of the formal theatre until she met Larry and, after a steamy courtship, married him.

Six years later, at the age of thirty-five, she was still unwilling to give up the time to have a child, by which time Larry had found in zen what she had with the stage. He had encouraged her in her theatrical pursuits at first, but finally came to the conclusion that she would never make it to Broadway. She was an excellent actress, often brilliant, but the city was filled with talent. He went to see her in anything she did, and later on she accompanied him to the East Side zendo for sitting a few times, but their interest in one another's involvement was not enthusiastic.

At times, they fought about it, Larry arguing that theatre was a narcissistic preoccupation and Eleanor countering that zen was a stodgy pastime. When he explained that his practice was actually very exciting, even terrifying in the way it squeezed every neurotic and psychotic element in the personality to the surface she retorted, "What do you think acting does? I know all about that kind of pressure. But I want to do something with it, not just sit on my ass and look at it."

The conflict inevitably affected their sex life. Larry found himself becoming quietistic in bed. During their lovemaking he began comparing it to sitting. While they moved together he would watch his breath, monitor his thoughts. Many times he drifted away, putting his body on automatic pilot, and it appeared that Eleanor didn't notice the difference. Also, as his practice revealed his deeper tensions to him—the tight stomach, the clenched sphincter, the knotted mind—he began to lose his capacity for thrusting. And it was then that Eleanor did notice, and started to compensate for his growing passivity. She became more violent, using her nails and teeth, trying to arouse him with dirty talk, and even for a while buying cocaine to provide extra stimulation. Each attempt was successful for a while, spurring Larry into a spurt of excitement, but before long his basic course reasserted itself. He was drifting away from shared eroticism into solitary meditation.

The marriage might have ended then, peacefully or explosively, had Eleanor not made the proposal that led to their living in the house outside of Woodstock where Larry was now shaving his head and reflecting on the nature of knowing. A man named Alec Moorman, legendary in certain theatrical circles for merging the principles of Gurdjieff with those of Stanislavski, was conducting a summer workshop in the town that had yet to be made famous by the rock festival which would define an entire generation. Eleanor wanted to study with him and suggested that she and Larry move there for three months.

"I can do my work," she said, "And you'll have all the peace and quiet you need for meditating."

He was at first startled and then pleased by the idea. He had a manager who could run the store. And whatever else happened, a summer in the woods would undoubtedly be rejuvenating for him and Eleanor. But what she said next stunned him. "Maybe it would be better if we had separate bedrooms while we're there," she said, and added, "And not make love."

Even though some part of him felt a sense of relief at her words, he was momentarily seized by panic, and he resisted the idea at first. Eleanor was sober and persuasive. "We've been married six years," she went on, "And you're all caught up in your zen thing and I'm at a point where I have to make a final decision about acting. After this workshop I want to know one way or another if I'm going to dedicate my life to it, success or no. And since you haven't been all there in bed for a while anyway, and we're both under pressure, why not give the sex thing a rest?"

"And what do we do in the Fall?" he asked.

"See if we still have a marriage we want to save. See if you want to go off to a monastery. See if I want to have a baby."

It was now a little more than two months since Eleanor had made her suggestion, and a month since they'd rented the small house in the woods half a mile away from any neighbor. After the first week of setting up, laying in supplies, exploring the land, they fell into a regular routine. Larry was up at five each morning, sat for two hours and then went in to shave and wash. Eleanor woke at seven and joined him for breakfast. He then returned to his day's sitting and studying, breaking in the afternoon to go into town for mail and errands. Eleanor worked around the house or went for a dip in a nearby swimming hole, and at eleven took off for her classes. She returned at six, made dinner, and they ate at seven. For the rest of the evening they watched television, read, or went into their separate bedrooms to do private work. Larry was in bed by ten, Eleanor usually stayed up until midnight.

Once they'd agreed upon the plan there had been no friction between them at all, except in the one instance of Eleanor's insisting that Larry bring his revolver with them. It was a gun he'd bought years earlier after his bookstore had been held up, but never had to use or even flourish since.

"What do we need a gun for?" he said. "The most dangerous thing around there are brown bears and they only grow to be three feet high."

"I don't care," she replied. "We'll be alone in the woods. What if some maniac comes by. I'll just feel safer having it, that's all."

He judged that it wasn't worth making an issue over, and they took it with them when they moved. It now lay, unloaded, the bullets in a small box next to it, in a drawer of Eleanor's night table, "a most unbuddhist object," as he referred to it.

Larry now sprinkled Witch Hazel on his scalp and washed out the bristle brush he'd used for lather. For a few moments he got lost in the scoured texture and whiteness of the sink and began to examine it minutely, the almost invisible network of cracks, the subtle shifts in curvature.

"This is all there is," he said to himself. "All the visions and fantasies, the other realms and universes, are all irrelevant. Only this is real, this moment, this perception. A bathroom sink is as much a source of wonder as all the heavens ever created." He stood for a while, his shaved head gleaming in the mirror, his brown gym pants sagging, his breathing sinking deep into his belly. Then he straightened up, cracked his knuckles and turned to leave the room.

But as he moved, his eyes picked up something that stopped him mid-stride. In the corner of the bathroom Eleanor had placed a laundry basket which was now, as usual, piled with rumpled clothing and sheets and towels. On top of the heap was a pair of Eleanor's panties. There was nothing odd about that, except that they were torn down one side, from the elastic strip around the waist halfway down to the bottom seam. Larry walked over and picked them up. He held them in his hands for a few seconds, a frown on his forehead, and examined them with the same purposeless precision with which he'd just looked at the sink.

Then, suddenly, harshly, a searing image burned through his brain. It had the hyperreal clarity of a snapshot taken with a flashbulb. He saw Eleanor's hips and belly and a man's hand grabbing the top of the panties. A second later, as though someone in his mind were showing a movie one frame at a time, he saw the hand tightened into a fist. And then movement, the hand yanking downward, the panties catching and, finally, tearing.

He blinked several times to erase the images and found himself staring at the actual garment with crossed eyes. He turned it inside out. The crotch was caked with dried secretions. He brought it to his nose to smell it. It was acid, with a hint of fruitiness. He sniffed again. Was that the faint aroma of sperm? He could not be sure. But how could that be possible? He and Eleanor had not made love for a month.

Larry felt something he hadn't experienced for years—the sharp clutch of jealousy twisting his stomach. In all the years they'd been together, he'd never doubted Eleanor's fidelity in the slightest. When they got married they decided to be sexually exclusive no matter what else happened. With her long hours at rehearsals and his days spent among hundreds of attractive women in his store, leaving back doors open would have been nerve-wracking for both of them. Especially since they were both exceptionally attractive people. Larry was a shade over six feet and before shaving his head had worn fine auburn hair to his shoulders. His body was slim, supple, and his blue eyes inevitably brought comparisons to Paul Newman. Eleanor was almost as tall, with skin that reminded one of pearls. With raven black hair, green eyes, a wide, thin mouth and large lustrous breasts, she continually commanded stares on the streets.

Now Larry swayed slightly, throwing a peculiar shadow on the bathroom wall. His knees trembled. And then, abruptly, he stiffened and smiled.

"Of course," he said out loud, *"Makyo."*

Makyo was the term in zen given to those projections and hallucinations to which people become prone when they sit for long periods. Sitting develops an enormous reservoir of energy and when that energy gathers sufficient force it floods the body and mind. The result is a magnification and intensification of any distortions imbedded in the muscular memory or in the conditioned circuits of the brain. The point of sitting is to develop an imperturbable balance and ease in the face of whatever grotesque, violent or pathological images and feelings arise. In a zendo, people often weep and scream and laugh, making the place seem more like a hall for primal therapy than for meditation.

"This is extraordinary," Larry thought. "Just because Eleanor tore her panties I was about to develop a whole melodrama in my head."

He closed his eyes for a moment to center himself, but the instant he did that the images began appearing again. The fist pulled the panties all the way down Eleanor's legs. Then it opened, and its fingers moved insolently over her thighs, stroked the thick patch of pubic hair, and started to slide slowly into the slippery chute between the moist, parted lips.

"Larry. Larry!".

The sound of his name being called out loud sent a shudder down his spine. He opened his eyes wide, straightened his back, and made a tremendous effort to pull himself back into his habitual focus.

"I'm coming," he said, his voice cracking slightly.

He put the panties back on the pile of clothes. After a second's hesitation he picked up some of the other items and threw them on top. He stared down for a moment, and then pulled the panties out and left them as they had originally been. His actions embarrassed him and once again he had to make an effort to shake free of his suddenly troubled perceptions.

"I'm coming," he repeated as he walked out of the sun-strafed bathroom.

— 2 —

Eleanor had already started water boiling. As Larry entered the kitchen she was standing at the stove, dressed in the jeans and t-shirt that had almost become a uniform since they moved to the country. As always, she wore no bra, something which Larry hadn't cared about one way or the other since his interest in eroticism had faded. But this morning he was struck by the intense sexuality of her simple presence, the long full legs straining against the thin blue cloth, her breasts shifting provocatively under the flimsy shirt, nipples accurately outlined. He mumbled a "good morning" and sat down at the kitchen table.

"I'm going in early today," Eleanor said as she poured water into the teapot in front of him. Eleanor drank coffee, and the aroma rising from the burbling percolator by the sink filled the room. After tea he would have yoghurt and fruit while Eleanor would eat nothing until lunch.

"Alec wants to do an all-day session," she went on.

Larry said nothing. He was still caught up in the fact that his feelings had almost gone out of control. His whole practice was geared to a single goal—attaining a still mind. And yet here he was, almost sullenly hunched over his morning tea, fearful of being dragged away by the wild horses of his imagination.

"Why don't you just ask her about the damn thing?" he said to himself. And instantly, he answered himself. "Because the panties are not the point. The issue is maintaining equilibrium."

"Voices and voices within," he thought. "Voices that ask and voices that answer, and thoughts that wear jackboots and throw other thoughts into conceptual concentration camps. And what about the master voice that observes the whole process and the sly awareness that observes even that voice? What about the idea that all ideas are incidental to understanding reality? And what makes me think that zen is anything more than one more relative viewpoint claiming to be absolute, except that a long line of masters have stated unequivocally that there is an absolute truth and that it be known with as much certainty as knowing the difference between hot and cold water."

"Your tea is getting cold," Eleanor said, pouring her coffee and sitting down across from him.

Larry lifted his head. "Oh? Sorry."

"What's up?" she asked. "First you're late to breakfast and now you're being glum. I must admit it's a relief from your usual morning mania, but is anything wrong?"

Again the temptation to ask, but the question froze on his lips. It suddenly seemed that it would sound silly to bring it up. What could he say? "See here, I want to know why your panties are torn." And then, abruptly, the spell lifted. He realized that if she did have something to hide the last thing she would do is put the evidence on display. Doubtless there was a simple explanation, and he decided not to inject a potentially awkward or ugly note into the atmosphere because he'd gone a little loony in the bathroom. Relief rippled through him. He smiled.

"No nothing," he replied. "Just some murky thoughts." He looked over at her. She was sipping her coffee. The sun's angle had shifted, altering the color and intensity of the light. Now it was less bombastic, and bathed the wood-panelled walls of the kitchen with a soft golden glow. Eleanor seemed surrounded by an aura. Her face was relaxed, the expression inward. Her beauty transfixed him for a moment, like that of a goddess appearing to distract a pious monk.

She felt the weight of his look and glanced at him, her eyes tender. "Dear Larry," she whispered and held her hand out toward him. Their fingers touched and he felt the current pass between them.

"An all-day session?" he said.

Eleanor turned her head abruptly to look at the wall clock. The electricity between their fingers stopped as suddenly as the extinction of a bulb when the switch is thrown. The moment that had just passed was the very breath of their marriage. As long as they had that contact, the relationship lived. In it they affirmed the pristine glimpse of the selves they had been when they first fell in love. Now he was aware of its fragility and of a quality in Eleanor he'd never seen before. When she removed her hand from his there was no trace of the lingering disengagement from that contact he'd always cherished.

"Hate to eat and run," she said lightly, standing up.

Off guard, he turned peevish. "Yes, you mustn't keep the great Mr. Moorman waiting."

She cocked her head, like someone hard of hearing, then faced him, her eyes opaque. "Mr. Moorman *is* waiting for *me*," she said, "Whereas you, I believe, have a date with a pillow."

His eyes narrowed and several seconds of dangerous silence passed. Then, in a completely uncharacteristic gesture, Eleanor passed her hand over her forehead and said, "I'm sorry, I didn't mean to snap at you." Larry stared at her. The quality of delivery, the mechanical nature of the gesture, was something he could not describe in any other way but to call it bad acting. And Eleanor had never "acted" with him, or if she had, it had been good enough to get by him.

To his astonishment, she went on in the same vein. "I guess it's just the pressure we're both feeling to find out whether this summer is going to work for us. And you seem so distant from me, so unreal."

He didn't know what her game was, if any, and his reply was tentative, probing. "I find it ironic that an actress would make a comment about someone else's unreality."

Abruptly as she'd stepped into role, she stepped out, and the Eleanor who replied was her normal self. "I know what's real," she said. "When my tooth hurts I see a dentist. When it's raining I use an umbrella.

When I look at stars at night I remember that everything's a mystery. What's the big deal?"

Larry looked at her quizzically. Her paraphrase of a master's famous definition of zen—"When I'm hungry, I eat; when I'm tired, I sleep"—perplexed him. He wasn't sure whether she'd read the line at some time and was now consciously playing on it, or whether her words were spontaneous. He had the distinct sense that she was somehow toying with him. Eleanor gazed back at him. "Why, Larry? Why do you have to sit on a pillow to find out what's real?"

The question, put so bluntly and in that context, left him momentarily speechless, although at another time he would have been able to reel off the five levels of awareness in sitting, and state the zen goal of having no goal, when the sitting is an end in itself. He shook his head, and Eleanor glanced at the clock again. "I'm sorry," she said, "But I really have to go." The apology had the ring of sincerity. "And I'm a little on edge," she went on. "Alec is heating up the training and it's taking its toll." She kissed him on the forehead. "Bye," she said, and walked out the front door.

Larry watched her go, noting how tightly the jeans clung to her buttocks, making her appear more naked than if she had worn nothing at all. He sat unmoving until he heard the car engine start, and with it a sudden crashing where a startled deer broke from behind a tree and ran into the woods. Then the crunch of tires on twigs and shale, and the rocking audible progress of the automobile down the hill.

With the departure of the machine, the woods returned to its own sounds, and within a few minutes Larry felt its spirit reassert itself. Like a fade-dissolve in a film, the image of Eleanor slowly disappeared as did all the questions and problems she represented for him. At such times Larry wondered how men got to assume the role of the movers and shakers of society. He saw Eleanor as a fierce vortex of implacable energy, and himself as a kind of litmus paper reacting to her influence. He wondered what she was feeling as she drove away from him, whether she was relieved at cutting loose from his relative stolidity and flinging herself into the world of action.

"What *are* we doing together?" he wondered.

It was his habit to take a brief walk after breakfast before beginning the second round of sitting, but this day had unsettled him enough to make him want to change his routine. He fixed a second cup of tea, then went into the living room where he dug out his secret cache of cigarettes. A year earlier, he and Eleanor had decided to give up smoking. He had stayed off almost a month and then found himself at a friend's house one night unable to refuse the offer of a smoke. The following morning he discovered that the habit was back. Eleanor had stayed off and he couldn't admit his failure to her. He could hear her, at key points in any argument, cutting him with, "Well, if you can't give up something as simple as smoking, I don't see how much good sitting on a pillow is doing you." So he became a secret smoker.

It was a role he found he enjoyed. The undercover vice made him feel like a man having an affair and successfully hiding it. In the cabin, he kept his stash in a classically obvious place, thrown carelessly in the back of the middle drawer of a writing desk which neither of them used. If she did happen upon the current pack one day, he could always feign surprise and suppose that it had been left by the people they'd rented from.

Now he drew a cigarette out, settled himself on the sofa with his tea nearby, lit up, and lay back to enjoy the sensations of smoking and sinning. Larry had been raised a Catholic and even though he'd intellectually outgrown its strictures, the training still shaped his emotional life, especially the pleasure of taking a bite of forbidden fuit. After trying to cleanse himself through therapy and LSD he realized that he would never be able to undo completely the conditioning that the church had wired into him and suspected he would always feel off-balance until he found a substitute.

Buddhism filled the bill perfectly. The Void was far superior to Jehovah as an absolute, Buddha far more rational than Jesus, and enlightenment more dignified than salvation. There was a world of difference between the lofty, transpersonal psychology of Buddhism and the cramped, fear-ridded dogmatics of Catholicism. Sitting zazen was formally the same as kneeling in prayer except that it was not done to curry favor with a petulant deity but to learn the realities of one's own character.

Larry sucked the smoke into his lungs, enjoying the searing sensation, the hint of pain, and the taste exploding raucously on his tongue. He blew the smoke out slowly, watching the yellow-white clouds expand in the air. Shifting his sense of scale, he imagined the shapes to be of enormous size, mile-long formations scudding with ponderous majesty across a vast horizon.

The question of why he and Eleanor were together now returned, but at a distance, like one of the smoke clouds drifting across the room. They'd fallen in love, which is to say, his desire had been aroused, and satisfied, and wanted more. He hadn't wanted to let go of her and marriage was the obvious way to hold on. Also, he'd reached an age and a place in his career where a wife and family made sense. And all of this was suffused with an unexamined romanticism, a yearning for the tantric union, the erotic transcendence.

They'd gone to bed together the night of the first day they met, and Larry shifted his weight on the couch as he thought of it. The cigarette had burned down to a stub and he ground it out in the saucer holding the tea cup. He sat back, his hands cupped behind his head, and drifted into a reverie. By now he would ordinarily have finished his walk and be sitting again, but the brief spell of renegade activity was proving too pleasant to terminate.

Larry had met her at his bookshop. She'd bought a very expensive book on mime and the following day, going over his receipts, Larry asked the manager who had bought the book. "A real looker," the manager replied. "If she comes in again, let me know," Larry told him, and was surprised when, a few hours later, there was a knock on his office door and Eleanor walked in.

"You wanted to see me?" she asked. She was stunning in tight black slacks and a black turtleneck shirt, the vitality and sensuality of her body overwhelming the tiny space. His visceral reaction was to want to jump up and run his hands over her a thousand times. The feeling flashed in his eyes and she hesitated a few seconds before stepping all the way into the room.

"I was curious," he said. "That book's been on the shelf for two years and I wondered who finally picked it up. Mel told me you were a looker and that made me even more interested in meeting you."

"A looker?" she said, her tone arch but her smile wry.

"It's a feeble word," he replied, "To describe *you*."

"And? Is your curiosity satisfied?"

"No. Now I want to know more about you. Forever."

She laughed. "You bookstore guys really have a line," she said.

Finally, she came all the way into the room and sat down. They talked, but the words were unimportant. The chemistry was there, that unmistakeable agitation of molecules and atoms changing the balance in the blood and the homeostatic humming of the brain. As she put it some ten hours later, "It's not too often I get the urge to wrap myself around a man I've just met, but the minute I saw you I knew it was going to happen."

"And you didn't play coy."

"I'm an avant-garde actress, I don't do dated roles."

It was just about six months before they came up for air, and then the realization, always right beneath the surface, that the sheer hunger for one another's bodies and life stories had to be sustained by something broader, more social. Perhaps, it might be argued, that that is the point in any affair when the parties ought to kiss one last time, smile sadly, and pay homage to the truth of transience as the ultimate principle of existence. But they were in no mood for philosophical perspectives. They were torn between the still compelling vibration of first heat and the not yet crystalized bond of full union. They toyed with a score of fantasies, such as giving up business and career and going to find a tropical island, or living in Nepal, or simply moving to San Fransisco to plant their passion in a different soil away from all the familiar roots of family and friends and childhood city streets, to play Adam and Eve again, the first couple on Earth, capable of creating a new world.

In those early euphoric days of constant hand holding, of impatience when they were apart for more than a few hours, they might have made the leap, daring destiny with their love. But they slipped back into consensual reality, and he was drawn back into the orbit of his work and she into her classes and tryouts and performances. The magic was transformed into responsibility, and the wild flights of fancy were turned into sensible arcs of overlapping routines. In short, they settled down, honoring the flame of early passion by tending the home fire of affection, and when their eyes and fingers met from time to time with a special feeling, it was like laying a wreath on a monument to memory.

After their marriage, Larry had not seriously been tempted by another woman. He knew that a brief affair would produce only sparks, and that didn't interest him. A serious affair would produce another cycle such as he'd gone through with Eleanor, and he was unwilling to risk those kinds of waves in his life. Also, the idea of having a child with Eleanor kept his lust focussed. And so as relatively mild as their marriage and lovemaking became, Larry remained content. Until the wild soul of zen sang to him and captured his mind and, increasingly, his body. Then Eleanor had a rival, and not in the form of a woman. The thought of Eleanor's being unfaithful had never occurred to him, not until this morning.

He lit a second cigarette and sipped the last of the tea. He was frowning again. "All right," he said out loud. "Do I believe that Eleanor is seeing someone?" He was silent for several puffs and his brow cleared. "No," he continued, "The question is: do I want to believe that Eleanor is seeing someone?"

Having made the distinction, he realized that all his concern of the day masked a more fundamental issue, which was what was his real intention for September.

He and Eleanor had agreed that the summer was to be a trial period, giving them a space in which to make a mature decision in the Fall, but he had not really faced the possibility of separation, at which point Eleanor would indeed be sleeping with other men. The idea of that was painful, yet he couldn't mask the fact that a large part of him wanted out of the struggle, wanted to go to the zen monastery in Monroe, just fifty miles from where he now sat, and devote the rest of his life to peaceful contemplation and study. He saw quite clearly that if Eleanor were indeed now having an affair with someone, the decision would have been made for him.

The analysis was accurate, but the information was still skimpy. The whole thing might be nothing more than a kind of hallucination arising from the combination of intensive meditation and celibacy. He felt a vein in his temple throb. Having two cigarettes in a row threatened to give him a headache and he put out the second one and sank back onto the couch with his eyes closed. However, he hadn't had more than a few seconds to take a deep breath when the projector in his brain started throwing images on the screen of his mind again.

This time there were no stills. He saw Eleanor as she'd been when she left a while earlier, only instead of driving to Alec's she is going through town, toward Saugerties. She turns off on one of the side roads and stops in front of a two-storey house. The front door opens. A man walks out. He is in his early forties,

vaguely European looking. Eleanor runs toward him.
He puts his arms around her. One hand slides down
to her waist, below her waist, cups her buttocks.

Larry opened his eyes and stared fiercely at the
ceiling, but the film continued inside his skull, under
the dome of his shaved head, even as he watched a fly
walk upside down across one of the wooden beams
holding up the ceiling. Now the man is lying on a bed,
naked. Eleanor is stretched out on top of him, wearing only her panties. Her face is buried in his crotch.
A close-up. Her lips are stretched taut around the
thick veined phallus. It is pulsing. The sperm is spurt-
ing out. Eleanor is sucking, swallowing, making
muffled whimpering sounds.

Larry sat bolt upright, his face contorted. He was at
the limits of his capacity to absorb the fantasy. But the
images were out of control. The mental power he'd
accumulated from so much sitting was far stronger
than he'd realized. His mind was like a rapidly over-
heating nuclear reactor.

He stood up and walked to the front door, wanting
to get outside, but the images only grew sharper. This
time Eleanor and her phantom lover are embracing
tightly. She is pushing herself against him, grinding,
kissing him hotly, wetly. His hand slides down. His
fingers are impatient. He pulls and yanks, and the
panties tear. The both look down, astonished. And
then they laugh. Eleanor reaches down and takes
them off.

"I'd better be careful," she says. "My husband is

pretty unconscious but he isn't completely in a coma yet."

"Why don't you leave them on his zen pillow," the man says. "That might wake him up."

Larry flung open the door and stepped into the bright morning sunlight. At once he felt better. The pictures in his mind faded. He looked at his hands and realized his fingers had been trembling. He leaned against a tree and felt the perspiration drying on his forehead.

"So that's what they mean when they talk about the power of *makyo*," he thought. "I never imagined it could be so fierce." And then he grinned, for it suddenly occurred to him that the whole episode was nothing other than proof that his practice was bearing fruit, that the zen-induced crisis of doubt was beginning to pervade his entire system. And he saw the logic of the unconscious mind's choosing Eleanor as the symbolic demon.

As he went back indoors, he concluded that there was no point in continuing to wonder about Eleanor's fidelity. She was or she wasn't, and he'd find out or he wouldn't. The important thing was to concentrate on his work. He picked up the teacup and saucer and took them into the kitchen to wash them, and then went out to the woodshed which he'd fixed up for meditation.

It held nothing but a mat and pillow, incense holder, gong, and a small statue of Buddha. He lit a stick of incense, did nine prostrations, and sat on his pillow. He swayed back and forth until he found his balance, then struck the gong three times. And by the time the vibrations had died down, he was in the correct posture, legs folded in full lotus, hands cupped below his navel, spine erect, eyes lidded, his awareness on the breath moving in and out of his lungs.

Larry continued another day of sitting, following a tradition that had been going on unbroken for at least two and a half thousand years.

— 3 —

Larry was sweeping the kitchen floor when Eleanor returned. She nodded her hello and without a word went into the bathroom to shower. He recognized her mood. She was irritable and edgy, a state which, in the old days, Larry would have transformed by making love to her. Now he just watched her sweep past, as he would storm clouds sailing past a distant mountain top.

He felt extremely calm. The day's sitting had been particularly rewarding, the last two sessions given over to a practice called *shikan taza* in which all devices, even watching the breath, are put aside, and one does nothing but "strike the seat," assuming an attitude of permanence and nobility like that of a majestic pine. It required extraordinary concentration and after each session he was sweating heavily. But it had the effect of a steam bath, purging him of his poisons, returning him to a sense of himself, free of the turmoil of relationship.

He finished tidying up the room and Eleanor returned wearing a white kaftan. She made dinner without talking, tossing pots and pans about carelessly while he set the table. Her mood was testy. They ate in silence, a dinner of brown rice and steamed vegetables. He buried himself in a book while Eleanor fidgeted in her chair and sighed explosively from time to time.

When they finished, she went into the living room and turned on the television while he did the dishes. When he joined her she was sunk deep in the easy chair watching Captain Kirk impose the Federation's benign dictatorship on a people who didn't want to be bothered but ultimately had no choice. Larry sat on the couch and watched with her until the show was over.

He was torn between wanting to retreat to his room and finding out if something was really troubling Eleanor. If her mood were volatile enough, whatever he did would spark an explosion. If he left her for the evening she might accuse him of being uncaring, and if he did speak to her she might snap at him for meddling. And the morning's upheaval and his subsequent lapse from discipline was an experience he didn't want to repeat.

"Finished watching?" he said when the program finished.

She nodded.

"Mind some music?"

She shook her head.

He flicked off the television and put on some Mozart quintets, following the advice of a friend who was fond of saying that one can never go wrong with Mozart. As the music began to fill the space, Larry sat on the couch, curled his feet under him, and began reading again. His attitude was one of showing that he wanted to make contact, but was also ready to efface himself entirely for as long as that was necessary. It was a particularly gratifying role, that of the Attentive and Understanding Husband, and it reminded him of a time when they had spent silent evenings together without the need for any posturings.

As he read, the tension seeped out of the room, and after almost half an hour, Eleanor stirred. Her face was now relaxed and her eyes clear and warm. "Want some tea?" she asked.

"Sure."

They looked at one another and there was a palpable feeling of affection between them.

"How about a game of Scrabble?" she asked.

He smiled in a way that was special to such moments. The game was one of their sacred rituals, a totem that served as symbol for the fundamental meaning of their marriage. It had no more or less significance in itself than a communion wafer or a black pillow; its value came from what they invested it with, and how they honored its function. Offering to play was always a sign of complete cessation of any hostility and the dropping of all residual bad feeling. Accepting the offer meant that the other had wiped the slate clean also. Neither of them had ever betrayed the good faith of the ritual by using the safe space to recommence warfare.

Larry set up the board while Eleanor made tea, and

by the time she was sitting across from him and the steaming cups were scenting the air, the room was cozy once more, now a nest for a man and woman who loved one another and were basking in the security of their hard-won relationship. In a marraige of any duration the sweetest moments are those when the two look at each other across the divide of the constantly yawning chasm that opens between them and find that they are still both there, still in contact and, against all odds, still bound in the embrace in which they discovered one another. This seemed one of those moments.

It was a scene so utterly perfect that it ran the risk of slipping into a parody of itself, the way Norman Rockwell's paintings hint at a well-masked dada sensibility underlying his vision. If Larry and Eleanor had been living a more normal married life, afterwards they'd have gone out to lie on their backs and look at the stars and be lost in the wonder of space in which all human aspirations, all the teachings of wise men and yearnings of soulful women, are seen as having no more importance than the sound of wind through the trees or the twitchings of the wings of a solitary butterfly among the flowers. Then they certainly would have made love on a rough blanket in the chill mountain air.

They sipped tea and spelled words and kept score and, at one point, Eleanor looked up with a mischievous smile and said, "You're going to hate me." When she said that it meant she had something like a Z on triple-letter square with the word itself perhaps counting for a double score. He was thirty-four points ahead but knew that the lead was temporary. Eleanor was a keen player and their lifetime record had her winning about sixty percent of the games.

His eyes played idly over her face as she looked down at her letters. She was, he realized again, an inordinately beautiful woman. The warmth of his feelings for her flushed through him as he recalled how long he'd known her and through how many changes. He was about to lean across the board to kiss her when some discrepancy in her appearance arrested his attention. He wasn't sure what it was, except that an intimation of horror caught at his belly, coupled with the kind of vertigo a person feels in a commonplace dream that's just about to turn into a nightmare. And just as he was about to take a breath, he saw what was different. The locket around Eleanor's throat was missing.

"Your locket," he said, his voice suddenly cracking.

It was a piece of jewelry he'd bought for her on their honeymoon, and there had not been a single day since then when she had not worn it. It fastened with a specially devised latch that could only be opened with a tiny key. He realized that he must have been aware earlier that she didn't have it on, but was only just now registering the fact. Seeing her without it was like seeing her without eyebrows.

Eleanor put her hand up to her throat. "The locket . . .?" she repeated. "I don't know . . . I'm sure I had it when . . ." She broke off.

"When what?"

Eleanor looked away, over Larry's shoulder, her face a playing field of emotions. Then she looked back at him, her expression composed. "When I took my clothes off," she added.

Caught leaning forward about to kiss her, he drew back. "Do you want to tell me about it?" he asked, surprised at the timbre of composure in his voice.

To his amazement, she smiled. "Well, of course, darling," she replied, chattily, as though she were about to describe some shopping she'd done that day. "It was nothing. Part of the workshop today involved working in the nude."

His brain jammed. Expecting to be told the story of her infidelity, he was instead tossed an explanation that was at once more innocent and more outrageous than that. He found himself reacting more violently than if she'd actually described a torrid scene with another man.

"In the nude!" he shouted.

"Why yes," she said. "Don't tell me you're going to be shocked over a simple acting exercise. After all, there were fifteen people there. It's not as though I were alone with a man."

"You mean you took your clothes off in front of fifteen people!"

"Well they were all naked too."

Larry was off balance. His anger was directed not at what he was hearing, but at what he'd expected to hear. But since he couldn't make any reference to the latter, his feelings about the former were caught in a vise.

"What about Alec?" he shot out, wanting to find some target. "Was he naked too?"

"Why no," she answered, her tone registering surprise that Larry would even ask such a quesiton.

"Well that must have been titillating for him, to have fifteen naked people cavorting in his living room."

"Oh for God's sake, Larry, Alec is in his sixties."

"What did you all do, touchie-feelies?"

Eleanor was about to reply, then hesitated, and smiled again, "Oh, you're just being silly. I believe you're jealous. Which is very flattering after all the deadpan you've been practicing."

He felt the advantage slipping from him and he returned to his original question. "So what happened to the locket?"

A look of hurt came into Eleanor's eyes and her lower lip trembled, as though she were about to cry. "I don't know," she said. Larry stared at her. For the second time that day he had the feeling that she was acting, but acting badly, without her usual skill. "How can you not know!" he said.

"We . . .," she began again, "We each had to stand alone in front of the group completely naked. And when it was my turn someone pointed out that I wasn't completely naked, that I had the locket on."

"That's idiotic," he interjected.

"Not really. That locket is more important to me than any piece of clothing I own and I knew that while I was wearing it I wasn't doing what Alec wanted, which was for each of us to stand without any defenses or identity in front of the others." Her eyes misted over. "Then, later, when we all got dressed, I must have forgotten to put it back on."

"Forgotten," he said, in a tone of voice a man might use whose wife forgot her baby in a shopping basket at the supermarket.

"It's got to be there," she said, her voice now louder, more strident. "I'll get it tomorrow. It's no big deal." She'd switched from sorrow to anger without missing a beat and Larry wondered once more if she were in some way toying with him.

"No," he said, injecting intimations of infinite sadness into his voice, "It's no big deal."

"Oh Larry," she moaned, all at once the essence of motherly concern. She got up, moved around the table that held the Scrabble board and knelt on the floor in front of him. She took his hands in hers and kissed his fingers. "I'm so sorry. I don't know how I could have done such a stupid thing. It's just that in the excitement . . . well, I can't make excuses but please try to understand. I should never have taken it off, but when Roger pointed it out . . ."

"Roger? Who's Roger?"

"One of the men in the group."

"That's right," he said, so low she could barely hear him. "The men in the group. It must have been nice for them."

Eleanor pulled away from him, stood up and walked over to the fireplace. She struck a pose of challenge, one hip forward. "It wasn't like that," she said.

"Wasn't it?" he said, his control slipping. He was at

the edge where it is still possible to pull back from the emotion that was welling inside him, but he couldn't resist the plunge. He tasted anger and jealousy, feelings he'd not known for a long while and, like a long-time vegetarian sitting down to a steak, was surprised that his taste for such meat had not diminished. He got up from the couch and walked to the other side of the room, away from Eleanor, as though he were afraid that proximity might inspire violence. A sudden furious hunger for a cigarette stabbed at his chest. But when he turned to face her, out of the corner of his eye he saw an apparition that seemed as real as the wall he was leaning against, a black-robed monk sitting on the couch with his face buried in his hands. Larry blinked and stared, and the mirage resolved itself into shadows and bits of the furniture.

"What's wrong?" Eleanor asked, "You're face just went all white."

"What's wrong? I may be going mad, that's what's wrong. And your standing naked in front of a bunch of men isn't exactly what I need right now." A new thought kicked in. "But then they were naked too, weren't they. So you got to see how all the boys were hung."

"Right Larry," she said, and her voice was so calm, so rational, that it made him feel suddenly embarrassed. "That's what the exercise was for. To get us in touch with all the hidden sexual agendas, the agendas of excitement and shame. Alec walked up and down and told us to look, to stare. 'Drink it all in,' he said, 'And find out what you're really feeling. Are you turned on? Do you want to have an orgy? Or do you want to crawl into a closet and hide?' And he made us stay at it until we all came clean about what was going on inside us."

"So clean you forgot to put your locket back on."

"Oh God, Larry, I'm sorry," she cried out, and once more underwent a startling shift in mood. Again she was tearful. They stood facing each other for almost a minute, and then she went toward him, slowly, almost shyly. When she was close enough to touch him, she stroked his cheeks with her hands. "I know how much it means to you," she said, "But it isn't lost, I promise you."

He put his arms around her and held her tightly. He remembered the day they'd bought the locket, at a small shop in Paris, and the way the saleslady had smiled when she learned they were honeymooners. He could still see the scene in perfect detail, the locket lying on a dark blue satin cloth, the key next to it.

"The key," Larry thought. "The locket only comes off with a key."

There was no change in his body, in the way he held himself or embraced Eleanor, but his mind became cold and clear. Eleanor kept the key in a sandalwood box on her dressing table, and if she had not known in advance that she would be asked to remove the locket during her acting exercise, she would not have brought the key with her. Which meant she couldn't have taken the locket off without snapping the chain, which he was certain she wouldn't have done.

"So she didn't leave it at Alec's class," he concluded.

In that instant of placid panic, Larry reached for whatever would comfort and sustain him, and recalled the zen teaching that whenever a thought arises, one should not be absorbed into its content but look to its source. All thoughts, pleasant and unpleasant, troubling and consoling, should be treated equally, merely as manifestations of mind, and it was to mind itself that one should pay attention.

He removed his arms from around her back, squeezed her shoulders once, and smiled at her. "You're right," he said. "I'm being foolish. Of course it'll turn up tomorrow."

She kissed him lightly on the cheek. "Why don't I make some more tea, and then we can finish the game. I'm going to beat you, you know."

"We'll see about that," he replied.

She went into the kitchen and Larry sat back down in the easy chair. He wanted a cigarette very badly now, but there was nothing for it. He leaned back and closed his eyes, the vein in his temple throbbing again. This was the first time that the ritual of their board game had been marred and by something that had the impact of a terrorist bomb in a restaurant. He took several deep breaths and then felt a palpable click in his mind. At once, the screen on which he'd seen the images that morning lit up, and again he saw the man's hand. He let out a small whimper when he realized that it was the *same* hand, that he *recognized* it. But this time it was not at Eleanor's waist, it was at her throat.

"What's this?" he asks, fingering the locket.

"Something Larry gave me on my honeymoon."

"Take it off."

"Why."

"I don't want anything of his on you when you make love to me."

"He'll notice if I don't have it on. He's not that dizzy."

"You can put it back on when you leave here. If you leave here. Why even go back to him?"

"I promised him the summer. I owe him that."

"So long as he's not touching you."

"No worry about that."

The hand moves down then, brushing over Eleanor's breasts, stopping, cupping them one at a time, squeezing, and then taking one nipple between thumb and index finger, pinching. Eleanor gasps, then sighs.

"Take it off now."

"I can't. It only opens with a key. I don't want to break it."

"Next time, bring the key."

"Yes."

Larry opened his eyes. It was clear to him that today had been that next time. Eleanor had brought the key with her, opened the locket, and when she left, made forgetful by passion, had driven off without it. But even as he accepted the accuracy of that conclusion, he realized that the whole idea might be a form of hallucination. Would Eleanor invent a story about a nude acting exercise, something that Larry could check on very easily? Of course, he'd never followed her tracks before and she could assume he wouldn't do that now.

He shook his head. As possibility and probability intertwined and faced off, he wondered why he was caught up in such a melodrama to begin with. He contrasted his current state to what he'd felt after his last sessions of sitting earlier in the day. That was all lightness and golden awareness, laced with clean, intense concentration. This was darkness in turmoil and a beckoning ambiguity.

"Can there be something to the idea that a woman is an impediment to a man's realization?" he thought. He remembered one of the first arguments he and Eleanor had had about Buddhism. He'd given her some books to read and her response had been to point out the overwhelming male prejudice in it and the derogatory statements made about women. Larry defended the offending patriarchs and masters, claiming that they were just using the idiom of their time. But he had no satisfactory reply to Eleanor's question as to why supposedly enlightened men didn't rise above the prejudices of their historical period.

He rubbed his eyes and sat up straight at the edge of the chair. Whatever the truth of these matters, the one thing he didn't want was a recurrence of the erotic images that had already seized his mind several times. He knew that if they were indeed *makyo*, he would have to endure them, and worse, before he broke through the blockade they represented. And he decided he had to have a reality check before he encountered those demons again.

Eleanor walked back into the room, carrying the teapot. Larry looked over at her and smiled. "Ready to be beat?" she said.

"How do you know I didn't look at your letters while you were gone?"

"Because I know you don't cheat." She sat on the couch and poured their tea. "And besides," she continued, "It wouldn't help you anyway. I'm still going to make the same score."

"O.K.," he said, "Let's see what you've got. And then, casually, offhandedly, asked, "By the way, how did you get it off?"

"Get what off?"

"The locket."

"Why with the key, of course."

"But don't you keep that in that trinket box of yours?"

"Not for a long time. I used to take the locket off when I went to the gym, especially when I got a massage. I started carrying the key with me in my purse and since we moved here haven't got around to putting it back in the box. It's a lucky thing too. Otherwise I wouldn't have been able to do the complete exercise today." She gazed at him quizzically for a few seconds. "What *have* you been thinking?" she said, smiling at him brightly.

— 4 —

It was an afternoon of perfect stillness. The perfume of earth and flowers made the air heavy and even the droning of insects and flap of birds were absorbed into the timeless stretch of the day. Larry sat unmoving. He might have been a tree stump or a rock. Only the deep, regular rising and falling of his belly indicated that he was alive. His breath entered and left his body silently. His brain was quiet. Small animals and even a family of deer passed by, within feet of where he sat, and took no fright.

He'd awakened that morning at complete peace with himself. He and Eleanor had finished their game the night before, then gone out to look at the stars. They stood for a long time without speaking, his arm around her shoulder, her arm around his waist. And when they went inside and kissed goodnight, he came very close to going into her room with her, taking the evening to its logical conclusion. But he hesitated, and she did not make the suggestion, so they slept apart once more. At breakfast, she was playful and even cuddly and when she left for her class at eleven Larry was feeling that it might be possible after all to have the best of both worlds.

It was Sunday, the day that Larry did his sitting outdoors on a small meditation platform he'd built a few hundred feet from the house. Many zen teachers had warned against sitting in too pleasant an environment, arguing that beautiful scenery or the vitality of nature could prove a distraction from one-pointed concentration, but he enjoyed the change, discovering on most days that being among the trees even sharpened his focus.

By his fifth session of the day he'd entered a state of pure awareness, in which his body was not distinct from the consciousness and spirit of the forest itself, and he experienced no difference between inside and outside. The far murmur of the stream, the heat of the sun and the snapping of twigs as animals went on their rounds became one with the beating of his heart, the circulation of his blood and the voluptuous rush of breath in and out of his lungs.

It was for him the perfect ideal of sitting, the fulfillment of the vision he'd seen when he first visited the East Side zendo, a converted town house where some two hundred people gathered one night a week for meditation. At one end of the long narrow hall sat the master, as firm as a stake driven deep into the ground. At the other end were the attendant monks, in charge of keeping the incense lit, hitting the huge temple gong at the proper moments, and directing traffic during the periods of ritual walking. By then he'd read a dozen books on zen and tried sitting on his own for a few months, and was still at the point where the posture produced cramps in his legs and sudden fits of anxiety in which he seemed to have forgotten how to breathe. But by the third hour of sitting at the zendo all difficulties fell away. The sheer brute force of so many people's gathering together in such fierce concentration flushed out his nervous system.

He was also intrigued by the unusual quality of intimacy the practice inspired. Sitting for several hours with so many people in stillness and silence made anonymity a form of closeness. The strangers on either side of him remained strangers in the technical sense, and yet when he left the hall he felt surprisingly connected to them. He knew they had gone through exactly the same experience he had, and the idiosyncratic forms of their personalities, attitudes, thoughts and feelings were irrelevant to the fact that they were all sharing a profound view of reality. They were all dedicated to the belief that sitting in zen is the expression of life in its purest form.

After that night he went once a week for six months and then joined the group formally. At that point he was allowed to go to dawn meditations and on several evenings on which the general public was not allowed. Eleanor had encouraged him then, glad that he'd found some "outside interest" to match her own involvement in theatre. And so he was drawn in, unconsciously at first and then with growing awareness that nothing in the world, not even Eleanor's embrace, quite matched those moments when the huge hall resounded with the deep, throbbing chants of the *sangha*, and the great gong sounded its reverberating call, and the incense lifted the spirit, while mind and body sank like a stone into wordless understanding.

It had been a straight path from those early experiences to this moment of sitting alone in the woods. Through it all he'd had to manage the details of daily life, the business and the social scene, taxes and emotional traumas, and above all, Eleanor. His friends had at first kidded him about his involvement in zen, and when he'd shaved his head had smiled indulgently, commenting that if Larry had to go round the religious bend zen was certainly the cleanest of all trips to take. His transformation had been so steady that he hadn't realized how commited he'd become until it became obvious that even his marriage was being called into question.

Now, deep in his meditation, he felt disconnected from all the identities of his conventional life, and from all the manifestations of the human world, and so it took a few seconds for him to register that the sound invading the woods was that of a car coming toward the house. It entered his mind like a pin working through the cloth of a shirt and sticking into the skin, and when he recognized the familiar pitch of the engine, a thought formed: "Eleanor must be home early."

The image of her appearing in the emptiness was like a rock thrown into a pond, creating concentric circles of association, and his brain filled with a disconnected jumble of perceptions and memories, trees and wives, buddhas and playmates from childhood, physical sensations and lines from scripture. And just as he was integrating all that, melting it down in the crucible of his posture, the bell on the timer rang, indicating that the present period of sitting was finished. He blinked once, then bent forward touching his forehead to the ground, swayed from side to side, stretched, and stood up.

He was now supposed to walk for ten minutes, with a slow and measured pace, hands folded on his chest. But when he turned he saw Eleanor standing at the edge of the small clearing where he'd built the meditation platform. She was looking at him diffidently, obviously wanting to talk to him but not wanting to intrude. He was struck by her appearance. She wore a pair of very short white trunks, so brief that some of her pubic hair curled out around the crotch. On top she had on a white haltar which was unequal to the task of containing her breasts. The impact of such cultured sensuality on his unprepared eyes rocked his balance. She walked slowly toward him.

"Hi," she said.

"This is a surprise."

"I missed you."

"Was I supposed to be someplace?"

"No, silly. I mean I suddenly wanted to be with you. We were taking a break between classes and I missed you. So I took a chance that you wouldn't mind my coming home early."

They stood facing one another, a foot apart, both a bit awkward, until Larry reached out and put his arms around her. She fell against him and he held her tightly. He was feeling so strong and so clear, and she looked so appealing and vulnerable, that he was swept into the embrace and beyond it, caught up not only by the immediacy of her softness and solidity but by the memory of all the times they had clung to one another over the years. He recalled the night he was suffering from a dose of LSD that was playing havoc with his neurons and was standing at the window of their apartment wondering, with a mixture of sobriety and drunkenness, whether it might not be best after all to put an end to the miserable creature he was convinced he really was. Eleanor had come up to him and simply put her arms around him. His first reaction was to draw back but she held him close. He stiffened and tried to squirm away, and then succumbed all at once, putting his chin on her shoulder and letting himself sag against her. He felt not only the love of a wife then, but the warmth and protection of a mother, the comfort of footsteps approaching the cradle in the night when the infant's nightmares had awakened it. In that instant he experienced Eleanor as succor and ominiscience as well as passion and tenderness. He'd swayed and rocked and she had held him, for almost a quarter of an hour, until her breathing had entered his and driven out the sense of worthlessness. Later that night, when they made love, he vowed silently to himself that he would never forget that moment of her saving him.

But he had, and now, as they embraced in the forest, he became aware of just how far they had drifted apart, and wondered whether they could ever find that connection again. He was grateful that they could at least still have moments like this, when it seemed that the promise of their union had not died.

They parted finally, and held hands.

"Want to walk?" she asked, smiling.

"I was just going to," he told her. "But we can do it together."

"Do I have to put my hands on my chest," she asked, teasing, "Or can I just stroll along?"

"Come on," he replied, slipping one arm around her waist.

They walked to the swimming hole, a bend in the nearby stream that someone had dammed up to form a pool. Right behind it a huge grey slab of rock jutted up, large and smooth enough for several people to lie down on it. For three hours in the early afternoon the rock got direct sunlight and was a perfect place for tanning.

They climbed the rock and stood at the top. They made a peculiar pair, she in her provocative shorts and haltar and he in his brown robe and shaved head. It was obvious to him that Eleanor wanted to make love, and he was more than half inclined to get into the mood himself. But they were in such delicate balance that he was afraid that sex would inject a dangerous intensity, a skew of channeled electricity.

They sat down side by side and for a few minutes said nothing, letting the stream do the talking for them. Still filled with the calm of the sitting he'd been doing alone on his pillow, he opened to the excitement of sitting on the rock with Eleanor. There was no doubt that this was pleasant and engaging, but it had the feel of being a passtime, an idleness. And if it were to lead to sex, that too would be only an experience. Whereas zazen was a practice, the core of a worldview. It would be wonderful to have both, but if he had to make a choice at that instant, the decicion would probably be in the direction of meditation.

"How about a swim?" she said.

"Sun's gone," he replied. "And we don't have any towels."

"Fuddy-duddy," she said. "I'm going in."

She slid down the rock on her buttocks and took her clothes off. It was the firt time Larry had even seen her naked in well over a month and he stared at her as though she were a stranger. She stuck a toe in the water, shivered dramatically at its coldness, and then plunged in, letting out a loud scream. He watched as she thrashed around, then swam in circles for a few minutes, and finally climbed back onto the bank. Her whole body was covered in goosebumps.

"You're going to turn into an icicle," he said, standing up and walking down the incline of the rock to her, putting his arms around her and holding her until her trembling stopped. When her body heat returned, she disengaged and reached down to pick up her shorts. She slipped a hand into one of the pockets and pulled out the locket and key.

"You found it!" he exclaimed.

"Of course. And I want you to put it on for me like you did the first time. And I promise never to take it off again."

"Not even for a massage?"

"Not for anything."

He took it from her and stepped behind her. He slipped it around her throat and fastened it at her neck, locking it with the key. She turned to face him, took the key from him, and abruptly tossed it into the water.

"Hey!" he shouted.

"That's to make sure," she said.

"That wasn't necessary."

"No, but it was fun."

"I don't know what to say."

"Don't say anything. Kiss me you fool."

He smiled, bent forward, and kissed her on the mouth, then the cheek, then the ear, and finally nuzzled her throat. But when he pulled back he noted something that made him catch his breath. On the left side of her throat, just below the jaw, there was a pale reddish bruise, squarish in shape, and mottled. Larry didn't indicate by any sound or movement that he'd seen anything, but the perception startled him. The mark was faint, but unmistakeable. It was what used to be called a hickey, or love bite, back in the days when teenagers still restricted themselves to necking.

"Don't go off the deep end," he said to himself. "It could just be a rash or an infected insect bite." But even as he consoled himself, he couldn't shake the feeling of certainty that a man had put it there, perhaps even that afternoon. And if that were the case, then Eleanor's returning early and being sexy and chummy would perfectly fit the pattern of an un-faithful wife suddenly overcome with guilt and want-ing to keep her marital flank covered.

"You O.K.?" she asked.

"Huh? Oh, I'm fine," he replied.

"You worry me sometimes. Like last night. You suddenly stared into space and your face got drawn and white."

"It's just my *mayko* acting up," he said airily.

"Mak—what?"

"It's a technical term for hallucinations. Comes from all that intense concentration."

"Like what kind of hallucinations?" she asked, frowning.

He stepped back. "Oh, I sometimes see naked women in the woods," he said, his tone light. But Eleanor's response was serious. "I'm real," she said angrily. "Maybe you're confused about that but . . ."

"But what?" he asked, sure she was about to finish with, "There are other men who aren't."

"Nothing," she said. Then reaching down for her shorts and haltar and getting dressed she added, "Now your hallucination has clothes on."

"I'm sorry," he said, "I was just making a joke. I didn't mean to make you angry."

"I'm not angry. Just sad. I thought we might have fun this afternoon."

"You mean sex?"

"Is that a no-no for you zen boys?"

"Well you're the one who suggested we lay off for the summer."

"It was just an idea, not an iron-clad contract."

"I'm sorry," he repeated.

"Don't you have any desire for me at all?"

"I did, a little, a few minutes ago. But I thought it might be better if we stuck to our plan."

"I don't know much about zen," she said, "But I thought it was supposed to free you up, make you more spontaneous. Instead it's making you more rigid."

"That's just this phase of it. It's something I have to get through."

"And how long does this phase last?"

"I don't know."

"Longer than a summer?"

"Probably."

"I see."

He felt her withdrawing inside herself, the open and playful mood turning sour, and a chill got into his muscles that was colder than the water of the mountain stream. He wanted to reach out to her for comfort, but his yearning was matched by resentment. He felt it unfair that to the pressure of his practice he must also deal with pressure from Eleanor.

"Do we have to get into this now?" he said.

"No, of course not. I guess I'm a little randy and it's making me irritable. I didn't mean to lay anything on you."

He smiled. "Friends?" he said.

"Always," she replied, "No matter what else happens."

"Ready to go back?"

"Sure."

As they walked toward the house, though, he couldn't resist making one probe to find out just how far in right field he might be. "Have you been scratching that mosquito bite?" he asked.

"Which bite?"

"The one on your throat. There." He pointed to the discoloration under her jaw.

She put her hand on the spot. "There's nothing there," she said.

"It looks like a bruise."

He expected her to reply casually and was stunned when he saw a look of terror come into her eyes. She stared at him for several seconds and her face fell apart, like a thief's who is surprised at a safe by the sudden glare of a policeman's flashlight. Then, with an effort that he recognized as drawing on all her training and resources as an actress, she quenched the expression in her eyes and took control of her facial mask. What was most uncanny about the entire performance, however, was his startling certainty that not only her recovery, but her initial reaction was all staged.

"Oh, I was doing a scene this morning where my partner was supposed to be strangling me. I guess he pressed harder than I thought."

He continued looking at her. "What's the matter," she asked, "Don't you believe me?"

"Of course," he said. "I know how you thespians get carried away."

She cocked an eyebrow at him. "You're a fine one to talk, with your . . . hallucinations."

As they entered the house Eleanor was relaxed and cheerful once more, but Larry felt jammed up inside himself. He realized that while from the persepctive of his zen work he was progressing into the thicket of illusion and was glad about that, from the viewpoint of ordinary daily life, which was supposed to be the essence of zen, he was turning into a suspicious husband, and one who didn't know whether his suspicions were grounded in actuality or the products of his seemingly runaway imagination.

— 5 —

The next morning Larry and Eleanor were cour-
teous to one another over breakfast, but when Larry
began his sitting he knew it was going to be a bad day
for meditation. Theoretically, when the mind was
most in upheaval, one could do the best work, but the
buzzing in Larry's brain was too much for him to
overcome and he found himself drifting in thoughts
about Eleanor's possible affair and being skewered by
recurrent stabs of jealousy. He simply could not maintain his calm and even began fidgeting on the pillow.
He struggled with it until lunchtime and then decided
to make his run into town early. He'd skipped two
days and he needed to pick up a few things anyway.

He put on slacks and a t-shirt and rolled out the
motorcycle he used as their second car. It was a hot
day and by the time he had kicked the big Yamaha
into life there were perspiration stains at the small of
his back. The engine started easily, and its roar
cracked the silence of the woods. He threw the throbbing metal beast into gear and took off down the back
roads until he came to the Glasco Turnpike, a two-
lane winding road that had originally been used to

haul material to and from the glass factory that was a major industry in the area during the previous century.

He rode out to Shady, which was little more than a scatter of houses given the designation of a town by virtue of the tiny post office, with its own ZIP code, that operated out of the living room of a seventy-year-old woman who'd lived in the same spot her whole life. He turned up Mead Mountain Road and went to the top of the three-thousand-foot mountain, rousing dogs and startling horses.

He stopped for a while at the chapel on top of the mountain, a tiny wooden church built by a renegade Catholic bishop in the 1930s, a cantankerous hermit who, ironically, became a folk hero when the first hippies moved to Woodstock and discovered him. Flattered by the attention, the man began saying Mass once more, but continued to define himself as an apostate, outside the dominion of the church. The chapel commanded a seventy-five mile view and Larry treated himself to an hour of just gazing into that liberating space.

He mounted the bike again and rode down the opposite side of the mountain and into the center of town which was composed of a postage-stamp green sporting a flagpole and a fountain and flanked by an eighteenth-century church and a string of shops and funky boutiques. The main street was crowded by Woodstock standards, the summer people having quadrupled the population of the place.

Larry parked his bike and made the circuit of Tinker Street in a half hour, pausing to gaze in shop windows and nodding to one or two people who he'd seen before and were familiar enough to greet but not to talk to. He found his post office box empty, and after he'd bought rice at the health food store, Ajax and toilet paper at the Grand Union, and cigarettes at the News Shop, he decided to be decadent and had two slices of pizza and a coke at the pizzeria. Then, his errands accomplished, he saw no point in hanging around.If he needed some social context in which to orient himself, this town could hardly provide it. He would have been much more at home in fifth century China.

"At least I don't feel so restless any more," he thought. "Maybe I can get in a good afternoon's sitting after all."

He rode back to the house, took a shower, and spent the rest of the day sitting. This time it went well. The mental and emotional distractions still arose, but he was able to breathe through them, to maintain his center of gravity in the *hara*, a few inches below the navel, and not be drawn into the machinations of his brain or his liver.

"This is home for me," he thought. "Everything else is confusion."

He sat for an extra period and when he finished it was after five o'clock. Feeling energetic, he went into the kitchen and began cooking rice and chopping vegetables, deciding to surprise Eleanor by having dinner prepared when she arrived. But by six she hadn't returned yet and Larry went out to the swimming hole to have a smoke.

When he got back to the house it was twenty to seven, and there was no sign of her. She was rarely late but he figured that Alec just might be holding them a bit longer than usual, and sat down with a book he was having trouble finishing, a dense study called *Letting Go* by a French scholar. It was a brilliant work but mercilessly opaque. He settled into the easy chair in the living room and sank into the writing like a heavy stone sinking into deep mud, slowly and inexorably.

By seven-thirty Eleanor still wasn't back.

The next hour and a half passed with Larry getting caught up in spirals of anxiety and anger, a pattern common to everyone in that situation—one doesn't know if the missing person is injured or being thoughtless. When his anger flared, he immediately imagined Eleanor in an accident and became concerned; as soon as he started to worry, he pictured her with another man and got into a rage once more.

When her car finally did pull into the driveway at nine-thirty, three and a half hours late, Larry was both relieved and furious. But when she opened the door and stepped inside, everything he was feeling was simply blown away by her appearance. Her jeans were covered with dirt, her blouse torn in several places, her hair dishevelled, and her face flushed. She leaned against the doorframe and sagged sideways.

"Christ," she said.

He rushed toward her and put one arm around her waist, supporting her, and together they walked to the couch where she sat down heavily.

"What happened?" he said, kneeling in front of her. "Are you all right?"

"Now I am. But I could sure use a drink."

He went to the cabinet and pulled out a bottle of brandy that had been left by the owners of the house and, stealing glances at Eleanor, poured a healthy shot into a small tumbler. He brought it to her and she grabbed the glass with both hands and drank half of it in a single swallow, her eyes closed, her fingers trembling.

Larry studied her. Now that he knew she was all right, he could stop being worried and pay attention to what was actually going on. Eleanor was obviously in a state, but not so much so that she'd lost the ability to make a dramatic entrance. For the third time in two days he had the uncanny feeling that she was acting for his benefit. And it was not something so straightforward as her lying to him; rather, she was attempting a role that was more complex, that involved other factors beyond mere deception. But he couldn't imagine what that might be, and had to remind himself that he was subject to vivid projections and could not entirely trust his perceptions or judgements.

Eleanor finished the brandy, gasped, fell back onto the sofa, and sighed. "Now I could really use a cigarette," she said. "I'm glad there are none in the house."

Larry turned and moved around the low table to sit

in the easy chair across from her. He was tempted for an instant to take the pack out, to offer her one, but then he would have one himself and he felt it would be too weird for both of them suddenly to be smoking together again, giving the scene the ambiance of more than a year before.

"What happened?" he asked when he'd sat down.

Eleanor shook herself and looked at Larry directly for the first time since she'd entered. "Oh my poor darling," she said, "You must have been worried."

He almost said, "That's the worst delivery you've ever had on a line," but instead replied, "I was upset, but that's all right. What happened to you?"

"Oh," she said, as though suddenly aware that she needed to give some accounting of her whereabouts. She took a breath and went on, "I left Alec's a little late and a few of us went to the Pub for a drink. I figured I'd get home about seven-thirty, but I had three martinis and we got into a discussion about one of the exercises we'd done this morning, and when I looked at my watch it was already eight." She looked at him pointedly and added, "If we'd had a phone I'd have called you," this last remark referring to the fact that it was Larry who insisted that they do without one for three months.

"Anyway," she went on, "When I started driving back I realized I was looped and even weaving a bit. When I got past the wooden bridge at the bottom of the hill I took a wrong turn."

"How could you do that?" he asked. "There's only one road and it goes right past our turnoff."

"I don't know. It was dark, I was drunk. The point is that I did it, and all of a sudden I was on a dirt road in the middle of the woods not knowing if it led to a house or what. And then the car stalled."

"Fantastic," Larry interjected, the sarcasm strong in his voice.

Eleanor ignored his tone. "That's not the word I used," she said. "The thing just went dead and wouldn't start again. Can I have some more brandy?"

"Haven't you had enough tonight?"

"For God's sake don't give me a tolerance lecture now!"

"O.K. Brandy coming up." He went to the cabinet and poured her another double. He watched as she sipped it. His feelings were in turmoil and he couldn't have described his state of mind. He was fairly sure that Eleanor was lying, but couldn't figure out why she'd come up with such a clumsy tale. Then again, it might be true, in which case he was getting excited over nothing.

Eleanor looked at him over the rim of her glass. "I panicked," she said. "I don't know why. The booze, partially. And we'd been working on violent scenes all day. But I got spooked. I was completely alone and it was pitch black in the woods. I couldn't even see any stars. I kept the headlights on for a while but was afraid of running down the battery. And then I began hearing noises, and I became convinced there was a man out there in the darkness, watching me, waiting to drag me out of the car, rape me, kill me.

"I couldn't just sit there any more so I got out and

started walking back to the main road, sure I was going to be attacked any second. I must have really been crazed because I decided to leave the dirt road and walk through the woods so the man couldn't get to me as easily. And then I started running, and completely fell apart. I tripped a dozen times and ran into branches and bushes.

"Finally, I got hold of myself and sat down and had a good cry. And when it was over I was all right. Still a little scared being alone in the woods at night, but not out of my gourd. I made it back to the car and when I turned the key the damn thing just started right up." She laughed, a bit hysterically. "Isn't that something? The sonofabitch just kicked into life."

She finished the rest of the brandy and he saw that she was indeed very drunk. He watched her as dispassionately as he would a woman on a bus. "That'a quite a tale," he said.

"A tale you call it. You think I made all that up?"

"Actually I don't. If you were going to invent a story as to why you were late I'm sure you'd have come up with something less complicated." Larry wasn't sure he believed that, but he was being led by his words, not choosing them.

"Why would I want to make up a story?"

"To cover the fact that you've been seeing another man?" he said, turning the statement into a question, keeping his tone light, and amazed that he was saying such a thing.

Eleanor stood up, swaying slightly. If she'd been startled by his oblique accusation, she gave no sign of it. "Boy, big help you are," was all she said, "Here I am all traumatized and you're having one of your mak . . . mak . . . whatever the hell they are." Then, abruptly, she yawned, and stretched sensuously, her body bulging and flexing. In her tattered state she looked like one of the disreputably succulent maidens in the Li'l Abner cartoon. "I'm going to take a bath," she announced.

"Don't drown," he said.

"I'm not that looped," she replied, her voice suddenly very sober and matter-of-fact. And when she walked off toward the bathroom her steps were firm and steady.

When she'd closed the door behind her he took out a cigarette and went out into the woods to smoke. "Maybe somebody will jump on *me*," he said to himself as he leaned against a tree and lit up. As the forest worked its spell on him he wondered if the real issue wasn't zen versus marriage or meditation versus sex, but nature versus people in any form. It occurred to him that perhaps the best thing to do was establish a hermitage, away from monks as well as women. "Out here," he said to himself," none of it matters, not Eleanor, not me, not all the Buddhas who ever farted into their pillows."

Through the trees he could see an edge of the house and the bathroom window, now showing a dim light from the inside. Eleanor had lit a candle for her bath, and he pictured her stretched out beneath the bubbles she always used. An atavistic impulse ran through him and he imagined himself stalking back into the house, kicking open the bathroom door, yanking her out of the tub and spanking her bottom until it was red, for all real or projected infidelities, and then taking her savagely on the bathroom floor, right next to the basket with the torn panties. In the fantasy he was a lumberjack, axe over his broad shoulders, bursting with vitality and seeing women as nothing more than wenches for quenching his lust. He took a deep breath and puffed out his chest, milking the image for all he could until an inner voice snapped the mood, so sharp that he was as startled as if a New York cab driver had suddenly honked his horn in Larry's ear. "Stop kidding yourself," it said. "You're a middle-class intellectual playing oriental games. Your old lady is sick of it and making it with somebody else and it serves you right."

"Don't believe it," another voice said. "You're a man whose trying to break out of the culture he was born into, heroic for trying something radically different. And your wife is insecure about it and trying to drag you back into her way of life."

"Which voice is right?" Larry said out loud.

"You decide," said a third voice in his head.

"But who am I?" Larry said to the night.

There was silence.

Larry knocked the flame off the tip of the cigarette, ground it out, and field-stripped the remaining butt. "This is great," he thought, "I'm standing out in the woods arguing with myself. I must really be getting batty."

As he started toward the house he glanced at the

bathroom window again and saw the shadows of the candle flame dancing on the glass, and without consciously deciding to, he walked toward it. Once there, trying not to make noise, he leaned forward and looked inside.

Eleanor was lying in the tub under a blanket of bubbles. Her hair was loose and floating, her nipples rising up from the foam, her feet wide apart resting on the far rim. Her eyes were closed and her mouth open. Her hands weren't visible but it was obvious they were in slow and regular motion. He couldn't see the details, but he knew that Eleanor was masturbating, fingering herself gently as she relaxed into the wet heat of the water.

Her whole attitude was one of peacefulness. She was not a frustrated woman seeking release but an already satisfied one recalling a former pleasure. If the scene in the bathroom had been a movie with subtitles explaining the action, Larry was sure he'd read that the leading lady was dreaming about a recent experience with some man, and obviously not the bald loonie peering in at the glass.

He was about to turn and leave when another of the powerful images that had started the morning before erupted in his mind. He sees Eleanor leaving the group at the Pub, and ten minutes later one of the men gets up to go also. It is done very discretely, but the others at the table exchange knowing glances. Larry had to grip onto the windowsill to fight a wave of vertigo when he realized it is not the same man he'd seen the past few times, and the possibility occured to him that Eleanor was not only having an affair, but screwing around in general.

In his head, the fantasy ground on inexorably. Eleanor and the man meet at a deserted spot. They get out of their cars and go into the woods. Eleanor stands against a tree, her breasts and hips thrust forward. The man spreads a blanket on the ground. She walks toward him, smiling. This is the first time with this man and she's excited by the newness of him. They embrace and kiss, and then she whispers in his ear, "We can't take too long, my husband is expecting me."

Larry blinked. The bathroom window was beginning to steam over and the actual woman lying in the tub was becoming indistinct, even as she began moving her hands more quickly, her face becoming taut, her mouth opening into an O, her toes curling. At the same time, superimposed on that reality was Larry's fantasy, or his peculiar perception of another reality, that of Eleanor lying on the ground, her movement and expression the same, except that instead of her fingers it was the rough, insistent movement of a man bringing her to orgasm.

Larry turned from the window and lurched away. He took a few steps and then caught his foot on an exposed root, stumbled, and fell face forward, cracking his shin on a sharp rock. The pain was unbearable and he curled up like a foetus, holding the injured part in his hands until the sensation subsided and became only mildly excruciating.

He lay there for several minutes, making no sound,

and when he did make a noise it was to whisper, "Hurt, hurt you bastard, Hurt!" After the mental and emotional confusion and anguish he'd been going through, pure physical pain came as a relief, something he understood and could deal with.

And then, without warning, he began crying. His eyes moistened, and tears began to flow, and finally he started sobbing, hoarse panting barks and moans that sounded like no animal who had ever walked those woods. He couldn't have said what he was crying for because in those moments his sense of self disappeared. And he only came to when he felt Eleanor's hand shaking his shoulder. She was kneeling next to him, a bathrobe over her shoulders, her expression a mixture of concern and contempt.

— 6 —

When he got to bed that night, after a shower, after
assuring Eleanor for the fourth time that he was all
right, he slept almost not at all. It was clear to him that
he was coming apart at the seams and had nowhere to
turn for help. Even if he'd been in a monastery, the
only advice or instruction he'd get from a master
would be to increase the pressure, to sit longer and
harder. He remembered how, during *sesshins,* after
twelve or fourteen hours of sitting, many people then
went on to spend the entire night on their pillows,
cross-legged and rigid in the chill darkness of the
zendo, pushing themselves to the edge of a breakthrough. As it was, his only support now was Eleanor,
and he could not confess his suspicions to her, expose
his weakness. She would comfort him, to be sure, but
would also lose whatever little respect she still had for
him. And what if she confessed an affair, or a streak
of promiscuity, could he handle that? And what if she
lied? Would he know? More importantly, he'd despise
himself for not being able to get through the crisis of
doubt to which his practice had brought him without
crying on a woman's shoulder. Of course, he wasn't

presently doing much better than that, lying on the ground and sobbing like a lunatic who's been locked out of his asylum, but at least he'd maintained some integrity of vision, and not made himself even more vulnerable to a woman who might be turning him into the town cuckold.

By the time the first birds began to stir, Larry had begun to drift into a hypnogogic trance. All the contents of his mind rose sluggishly from the bottom of his brain and floated up and down the dream canals of consciousness, like indolent fish in a lazy current. Then, all at once Larry was dreaming of fish, goldfish that gradually grew larger and rounder and darker, until they looked like meditation pillows, whose faces were all those of Eleanor in a score of guises, laughing, scowling, thinking, reflecting the voluptuous flushes of orgasm. And when dawn had played its hand and the sun had appeared, Larry woke up. He felt completely refreshed, without confusion or fatigue. Like a madman or a genuis, he'd awakened with a new idea, an equation the simplicity and daring of which was breathtaking.

"Eleanor is my *koan*," he said out loud.

The use of the *koan* was a relatively late development in zen, coming into vogue sometime around the thirteenth century. Usually it was an enigmatic statement by a master, or a bit of dialogue between master and student, or a seeming nonsense question, the most famous of which was, "What is the sound of one hand clapping?" In the Rinzai school of zen, the *koan* was central to practice. As one sat, one was supposed to be absorbed into it, to breathe it, to sweat it, and to let it pervade one's whole being throughout the day, in all activities, and even in sleep.

The master Larry studied with, however, was of the Soto school, which rarely used *koans*. As one teacher in that lineage put it, "Some people, when they sit, need something to occupy their minds, and that's all right. But the most important thing is the sitting." For Larry now to take on a *koan* on his own, without supervision, was risky. For him to turn Eleanor into his "irrational question" was extremely dangerous. But the notion gripped him with all the sense of rightness of a line of poetry, as well as making a kind of wild sense. It resonated with the long tradition in Buddhism in which women were seen as obstacles to enlightenment, except that instead of dealing with the problem by avoiding women, this would cut right to the heart of the matter, fusing his practice with his marriage.

Larry lay in bed until almost seven, skipping his morning sessions, and then dressed, washed and shaved, and went into the kitchen for breakfast. Eleanor seemed not to be up yet, so he set her coffee to perking and fixed himself tea. He was having his fruit and yoghurt when she walked into the kitchen, looking somewhat hung-over.

"Coffee's ready," he said.

"Thanks," she said glumly, not looking at him.

"Had a bad night?"

She poured coffee into her cup and sat across from him. "Considering that my husband seems to be having a nervous breakdown, not so bad."

"I'm sorry if I upset you." He smiled. "I just needed a good cry, that's all."

"Rolling around in the dirt outside the house?"

He shrugged. "You know how it is with emotional crisis. You don't always get to pick the time and place."

"I thought your sitting was supposed to get you beyond all that weak human stuff."

"Eventually. But first it's necessary to go more deeply into it."

She sipped her coffee silently for a while, then glanced up at him. "You're obviously feeling better this morning."

"I've thought a few things through."

"Glad to hear it," she replied, not masking the sarcasm in her voice. "Maybe I should try that. But then, I guess I'm still under the delusion that we're working things out together."

"I'm sure there are things you don't tell me," he said pointedly.

"What's that supposed to mean?"

"You tell me."

"You're getting weird," she said.

She went back to the counter next to the sink to pour more coffee. Larry looked at her, aware as always of her beauty which included not only the wild-child face and hot-woman body, but the gracefulness and sureness of movement born of many years of training for the stage. But for the first time in his life he was also seeing her as an impersonal vortex of energy, as a principle. As a person she could be maddening or delightful, affectionate or hateful, faithful or wanton, and he would be vulnerable to all that. But as a *koan*, she could do nothing that would not feed his insight, intensify his meditation.

She turned abruptly and caught him staring at her. "What's in that seething brain of yours now?" she asked.

"What do you mean?"

"Come on, Larry. I know you pretty well after all these years. And you look like you've come up with another one of your grand explanations. Are you going to share it with me or take it with you out to the woodshed where you bring all your real feelings?"

"I've come up with a new idea for my practice, that's all. It's just technical stuff. I'm sure it wouldn't interest you."

"I'm sure," she said, making no attempt to hide her displeasure. "But be careful."

"Is that a threat?"

Instantly her mood changed, one of those sudden shifts she did so well in a role, and it occurred to Larry that perhaps he served the same function in her worldview that she'd come to assume in his, that in the same way he saw her as a *koan* to be solved, she was treating him as a character to play against. But even as he formulated the thought, she walked over to him. "A threat?" she said. "What's wrong with you? I'm worried about you, I don't want to see you going round the bend. I figure you know what you're doing with this zen stuff, but sometimes I wonder if you aren't in over your head."

Once more he was thrown off balance, touched by the seeming sincerity of her tone, but at the same time aware that that might be an act, a screen behind which she was making her own plans prior to some unilateral move. He had no doubt that she cared for him, as he did for her, but the twin courses of their lives might either shred that or render it academic at any time. He found himself gazing blankly at her as she stroked his face. "Where *are* you?" she said.

He shook himself loose inwardly and took her hands in his. "Look," he said. "If I were a physicist or something like that, I'd be working on things in my lab that I couldn't really explain to anyone else. And they might be dangerous, but that would be my job. Please don't be worried. I'm all right. I just have to see something through."

"O.K.," she said after a few seconds. "I'm trying to understand."

"Thanks."

She stepped away from him and looked over at the wall clock. "I have another all-day session, so I've got to leave now."

"So early? It's not even eight."

"Classes start at ten. I think I'll take a drive down to the reservoir first and clear my head out."

"I don't want to feel that I'm driving you out of the house."

"Silly, it's nothing like that." She put her cup in the

sink, walked back to him, kissed him lightly on the lips, and went to the front door. "Take it easy today, all right?"

"Sure."

Eleanor turned and walked outside, and in a few moments he heard the car starting up and moving off down the driveway and over the dirt road through the woods.

"Maybe I will take it easy today," he thought when the house was silent again. He made more tea and went into the living room to get a cigarette. He sat on the couch for a while, drinking and smoking, letting his new appreciation of Eleanor as the central focus of his meditation turn around in his mind. At one level, it was insanity; at another, a possibly unique effort in zen.

He thought about the whole history of their relationship, remembering special moments that, in retrospect, seemed a kind of satori or enlightenment in their own right but which were always singular events, without continuity. He recalled a day they spent on a deserted stretch of beach on Fire Island, lunching on bread and cheese and wine, and then making love in the dunes. When they'd finished, Eleanor pointed at something a few yards away and shivered. It was a dead gull, its legs sticking out stiffly from the body, its neck an unnaturally graceful curve, its eyes closed. They went over and looked at it, both fascinated and repelled. "It's funny," Eleanor had said, "We were making love right next to it. Sex and death side by side." In that instant Larry had an insight for which he'd found no satisfactory terms until several years later. For him, then, all distinctions dissolved. Organic and inorganic, living and dead, sea and sky, all were one.

As he played back the scene, however, another string of images intruded on the peaceful moment of memory. These showed Eleanor by the reservoir, only not simply gazing at the water and surrounding mountains, but lying behind the stone wall where the rowboats were kept, with the man from the night before, in another brief tryst, this time before class. She is face down on the grass, her jeans pulled down to her knees, allowing her to spread her thighs only slightly, and her buttocks raised as he takes her from behind, his erection jutting out from the open zipper of his slacks.

But instead of being shattered by the vision as he was the previous times he suffered such erotic seizures, Larry only smiled. "The *koan* gets laid," he said out loud. He put his cigarette out and congratulated himself on his ability to make the distinction between his feelings for Eleanor as a woman and Eleanor as the concept that he had to transcend.

In seeing her as an abstraction he also distanced himself from certain human niceties he would otherwise have observed, such as respecting Eleanor's privacy. Following the logic of his strategy, he got up and went into Eleanor's bedroom. He realized that what he was about to do was ignoble, but like a politician defending the invasion of another people, he excused his behavior on the grounds of consistency with a principle.

The bed was unmade and the state of the sheets indicated that Eleanor had also had a restless night. On the floor by the side of the bed were the clothes Eleanor was wearing when she made her startling entrance, and he picked them up to examine them. The blouse did look like it had been torn by branches, but the jeans were dirty in only two places, the knees and the seat. Either she'd fallen twice, once forward and once backward, or else been kneeling and sitting, actions that suggested another scenario altogether. Next he pored over her panties. As with the pair he'd found in the laundry basket, the crotch was thick with dried secretions, so caked that he could discern fine hairline cracks in the surface, like splits in a mudflat abandoned by the tide and punished by the sun.

He was about to lift them to his nostrils to sniff them when he caught sight of himself in the full-length mirror on the closet door. He saw a tall bald-headed man in a brown robe about to smell his wife's soiled underwear to find evidence of her infidelity, and the sudden absurd image shook his resolve. He dropped the clothing back on the floor and arranged the pile so it looked as it had before he'd picked through it.

He glanced around the room. Nothing seemed out of the ordinary. He walked over to the dressing table, noting the array of homely items across the top of it . . . lipstick, earrings, jars and tubes of various facial preparations, some rocks she'd found in the stream. Then, gingerly, he opened the two side drawers, one at a time. There was nothing of interest: some jewelry, scarves, a few brassieres she rarely wore.

Next he opened the wide slim drawer above the space where the matching chair slipped in. At first glance he saw nothing but handkerchiefs and rolled-up tissues covered with dried cold-cream. He pulled the drawer out a few more inches and his eyes widened. He reached down and picked up a familiar object, a pack of Pall Malls, which had been Eleanor's brand when she used to smoke. For an instant he was puzzled, and then it was clear. Eleanor had a hidden stash also and, like him, had become a secret smoker. But even as he was registering the revelation, he saw something else at the back of the drawer, something that every instinct told him to leave alone. But he could not resist. It was a Polaroid photograph, lying face down.

He turned it over. It was a shot of Eleanor. She was sitting in a large armchair he didn't recognize, in a room that was unfamiliar to him. She was wearing her haltar and shorts, and one leg was raised over the side of the chair, making her prominent pubic bone the center of the picture. She had her hands clasped behind her head, raising her breasts. The effect was not lewd, but pleasantly sexy, like old Esquire magazine pinups. It was the kind of photograph a lover might take.

But it was also a shot that a friend in the acting workshop might have snapped during a break, and

Eleanor could always claim something like that. It looked recent, but she'd had the outfit for more than a year, and the photo could conceivably have been taken months earlier. As he stared at it, though, the skin on the back of his neck began to tingle and he was suddenly convinced that Eleanor had returned silently and was now standing behind him. He squared his shoulders, set his features, and turned around quickly. The room was empty.

He smiled grimly. He'd have felt foolish if she'd actually caught him there, but he didn't regret his action. He put the pack of cigarettes back and slipped the photograph, face down, behind it, then shut the drawer and, looking around to see that everything was as he'd found it, left the room.

"I've gone this far, why not take it further?" he thought. "If I'm to penetrate the meaning of the *koan*, perhaps I should pursue it. Perhaps I should pursue her."

He went into his room and changed into jeans and a shirt and put on a pair of socks and work boots. He was now moving outside anything that might be construed as zen practice by any orthodox master. But then, zen also had a tradition of totally unconventional masters who urged their students to be wild, to disregard the formal teachings and rituals, to find their enlightenment on the wing.

"Anyway, it's time I met the great Mr. Moorman," he concluded. He went outside, kicked the motorcycle into life, and rode down the side of the mountain, in search of he didn't know what.

— 7 —

As Larry maneuvered the winding turns, shifting and braking, he wondered at the wisdom of his impulse. He had no specific goal and didn't really expect to catch Eleanor at some indiscretion. Rather, he hoped to absorb some of the texture and mood of her life in the workshop, to pick up some clue, however vague, about her inner directions. At home, confronting her directly, he would only see the mask she chose to wear for him. But while she was involved with others he might peer into her from an angle. He was a bit nervous about just barging in unannounced, but Eleanor had told him early on that that would be all right since Alec thrived on unexpected developments.

He also wondered what Shido, the master who ran the zen center, would say to his current notion of treating Eleanor as a *koan*. On the occasion of his formal talks, Shido refused to deal with details of life problems. His only response to any situation was the recommendation to continue sitting. "This is our faith," he stressed, "That in sitting everything becomes clear and the power of the true self emerges."

Larry had tended to think such advice a bit simple-minded at first, until he learned of the enormity of Shido's own accomplishments. He'd run four monasteries in Japan, managing some two thousand monks. He came to the United States not speaking a word of English, and within five years had established a thriving zen center in the city and built a monastery in the Catskills. He'd had four books published and was honored as a teacher by leaders of most religious groups. He was also married and had three children. Yet he rarely spoke, and when he did it was to say only the simplest things. All of his achievements seemed to flow effortlessly from the practice of spending many hours each day doing nothing but sitting.

As Larry reached the bottom of the mountain, he realized that Shido would consider his present state of mind one of lunatic agitation and tell him to get back to his meditation room. "Well," Larry thought, "At least I'm sitting, even if it is on a motorcycle."

He turned right and headed toward the town of Phoenicia, some ten miles away. Eleanor had given him directions to Alec's shortly after she'd been there herself for the first time, and they involved a right turn into the hills that rise up from the river running through the village. From that point on he had to stay alert through several cutoffs until he was chugging along a dirt road that had no name. When he arrived at the large house, he pulled in among the ten or so cars parked in front of it and switched off the engine.

The house was far up into the hills, at least a mile from any neighbor, and almost that distance from the main road. It was one of those huge disjointed structures of about eight or nine rooms that must have been popular around the first few decades of the century. He walked up to the front door and knocked. Fifteen seconds passed with no answer. He knocked again, and again there was silence. Shrugging, he tried the knob and pushed the door open. He stepped inside and walked through a long foyer that opened onto a very large living room.

"Hello," he called out.

There was no reply and he stood there for a few moments wondering what to do when, through the wide glass sliding doors that made up almost an entire wall of the room, he saw a man darting out from behind a tree, pausing to look around in every direction, and running back into the woods. Larry waited to see whether any more apparitions would appear, and after a while decided to sit and wait.

Aside from a beat-up easy chair and two straight-back chairs, there was no furniture in the room. A dozen large floor pillows were strewn about and he decided to use one of those. He took off his boots, sank onto one of the pillows, folded his legs in a lotus, and settled in to see what might happen next. Ten minutes passed and Larry began to feel as though he were sitting in meditation instead of as in a waiting room. In that context, the strange surroundings and the fact that he was there in some undefined pursuit of Eleanor faded into the background and he was left with the pure awareness of his posture and breath.

He lost track of time and space and was roused

from his concentration only by the sense that someone else was in the room, and had been in the room for several minutes. He shook his head slowly, rocked from side to side, unlocked his legs, and looked around. In one corner of the room stood a man sporting a white beard and mane. He was short and stocky, with a thick chest and a full belly that bulged over the waist of his shorts. He was barefoot and holding a frosted can of beer.

"Bravo!" the man said.

Larry stood up. "I wasn't aware I was in a performance," he replied.

"In this house, everything's a performance."

"Really," Larry said, drily, a bit miffed at having been watched and judged.

"I'm Alec," the man said, coming forward and extending his hand. They shook hands and he went on, "You must be Larry."

"How did you know?"

"Eleanor's talked about you, of course. And who else would be sitting in a full lotus in my living room, with a shaved head yet?"

"True enough. But I wasn't performing."

"I'd say you'd reached the point where your only awareness was of your awareness, but that's still a kind of self-consciousness. And as long as any self persists in your practice, your pillow is still a stage on which you are mounting your act."

Larry's eyebrows shot up. Alec's perception of his quality of sitting and his knowledgeability about levels of zen practice was surprising. Alec smiled, at first a straightforward expression of friendliness, but then the smile changed until it was almost grotesque, looking as though the man who wore it had buck teeth. His eyes narrowed and, as Larry watched, Alec was transformed into an Oriental. "You are surprise' I speak your ranguage?" he said, imitating a long line of Japanese colonels who ran Hollywood concentration camps.

Larry laughed, the first time he'd done so in weeks.

"Would you like a beer?" Alec asked.

"I don't drink," Larry said at precisely the same instant Alec also said, "I don't drink."

"Am I that obvious?" Larry said.

"Everybody's got a role, right?" Alec replied. "It's just a question of spotting the premise, then deducing what would be consistent with the character. Pretty simple stuff, really."

"O.K., I'll have a beer," Larry said. "I wouldn't want to be too consistent."

"That's the spirit," Alec replied, and went into the next room where he could be heard rummaging about in a refrigerator. "Tell me," he shouted, "Before the others return and things get complicated, why did you come here today. Tell the truth now, or else come up with an interesting lie."

Larry smiled to himself. Suddenly he felt a liking for the other man, a sense of cameraderie, an intuition that Alec was someone who would understand perfectly anything Larry told him about his inner life or his problems with Eleanor. In the same instant, he wanted Alec to like him and to respect him. It did not occur to him that this was the effect the charismatic director had on everyone and was the reason, apart from his native theatrical genius, that made him such a powerful teacher.

"I came to see what Eleanor is up to," Larry replied, making the statement innocent and suggestive at the same time. But any cleverness he might have felt was cut short by the sight of Eleanor walking into the room, coming through the door Alec had left by.

"Why Larry," she said, "What do you think I could possibly be up to in an acting workshop?"

Larry's first response was chagrin at being taken off guard, then anger at being suckered. "Were you in the next room all along?" he asked.

"All along when?" she replied ingenuously. She walked up to him, her eyes twinkling, radiating good humor, put her arms around his neck, pressed herself tightly against him, and kissed him on the lips warmly. She held the kiss for several seconds until Larry felt the surge of response in his thighs and chest and tongue. Then, as though she were throwing a switch, she turned the chemistry off and stepped back, smiling pleasantly, as though she'd just shaken his hand instead of his libido. "What a nice surprise," she said.

"In my day we used to say, 'Look at what the cat dragged in'," Alec said as he came back into the room, a fresh beer can in hand. Larry took the frosted can from him and turned back to Eleanor. "I was just out for a ride," he said, "And I thought it might be a good day to pay a visit. I've been meaning to meet Alec."

"Not bad," Alec said.

"What's that?" Larry said.

"The interesting lie you just told."

Larry was about to protest that he was telling the truth when he saw what a trap that would be. He was lying, and Alec was exposing him, and the only way to handle the sudden seeming betrayal was with silence. "Cat must have got your tongue before it dragged you in," Alec went on. Larry felt distinctly uncomfortable, the space between the three of them thick with psychic challenge and danger.

Then Alec broke the mood by clapping Larry on the shoulder and saying to Eleanor, in the chiding tones of a teacher to his student, "Didn't you warn him?"

"Warn me?" Larry said, almost perspiring, holding the beer can stiffly in one hand.

"Anybody is free to visit," Alec went on, slipping his arm around Larry's shoulder, "But anybody is fair game."

"Fair game for what?"

"For the game we play here."

"You mean hide-and-seek?" Larry said, trying to inject mild contempt into his voice. "People running around in the woods and women hiding in the next room."

"Oh Larry," Eleanor said, her voice halfway between mock and real disappointment.

"No, no," Alec interjected. "He's right. That is the game. And sometimes we play it like children, pretending we're invisible behind a tree or hiding behind a door." He took his arm from Larry's shoulder and walked around him to the glass doors. "Sometimes, we hide from ourselves. And, to use language you are probably more familiar with, ultimately we seek the Self—capital S, of which, presumably, we are all chips off the old block."

Larry took a swig of beer, and felt an immediate rush from the unaccustomed alcohol. He glanced at Eleanor. She had her arms folded over her chest and was watching him quizzically. He looked back at Alec who regarded him like a benign uncle waiting to see if his clever nephew was going to be able to put the puzzle together. Larry realized that by barging into Eleanor's world unannounced he had also stepped in Alec's world, in which all social conventions were rendered transparent. He wondered how far the man would go.

"That's more Hindu than zen," Larry said, scrambling back into familiar territory.

"Oy," Alec exclaimed. "Such fancy shmancy. I used that language to make you comfortable, not to get into a discussion about religion."

"You prefer another kind of theatre," Larry said, getting into the spirit of the exchange. It was clear now that Alec was baiting him and, by extension, his practice. He realized that Eleanor must have talked about him and his "obsession" quite a bit to Alec, and the director obviously considered zen just another form of drama, and not a particularly fascinating one.

"Well," Alec drawled, "I don't call what I do theatre. Some of the people I've trained have done stage and screen, and a couple of them are pretty big stars, but that's not what I'm aiming for."

"What are you aiming for?"

"The bathroom," Alec replied. "I haven't moved my bowels in two days and now it's time. Maybe your meditation did some good after all." He moved from the window and across the room with exaggerated delicacy, as though he were trying to keep from rousing someone sleeping.

Larry was non-plussed. He didn't know whether Alec was actually going to the bathroom or circling around the house to make an entrance from the other side or simply fooling, with no purpose other than to have his peculiar brand of fun. Eleanor was beaming. "Isn't he fantastic?" she said.

Larry took a sip of beer. "He knows much more about zen than I would have imagined," he said grudgingly. "And he is amusing."

With his last word, Eleanor's eyes narrowed and glittered momentarily, warning him he'd been a little too condescending, a reaction he himself would have had if someone described Shido as "cute." Actually, he was a bit afraid of Alec and his superior attitude was a defense against his own tendency to let his guard down in front of the man.

"The others should be coming back soon," she said, changing her tone back to one of friendly neutrality. "Why don't we get comfortable? You are staying for a while?"

"Sure. I hope you don't mind."

"Why should I? You let me come to your zendo."

"It doesn't feel like the same thing."

"It might be a bit trickier here."

"How's that?"

"Alec was right, I should have told you what to expect if you came. He uses everything and everyone as material. He's really ruthless. And he makes us be ruthless too."

"How?" Larry asked, feeling his heart skip a beat.

"Let's sit down," she replied. They each took a pillow and sat four or five feet apart, taking the same casual distance as strangers or students in a class. She went on, "I suppose you could call the game we play hide-and-seek, but technically what we're doing is assuming a role without letting anyone know what it is. Then we have to maintain that, as an inner discipline, no matter what else we do, whether it's running around in the woods or even reading lines from Shakespeare."

"What's the point?"

"Well, you get to see that that's what we all do all the time anyway. That's the way life is, except that very few people are aware that they're acting, or that others are acting. This wakes us up to how we really are."

"And this makes you a better actress?"

"On the stage or in life?" she asked, countering his question.

Again Larry felt his heart flutter and he wasn't sure whether it was the alcohol or his recurring sense that he was very close to the edge of a mystery. He knew that something was being revealed, but he couldn't yet grasp its form. He saw that there were certain similarities between his practice and the metatheatre that Alec taught. The approaches were worlds apart in structure but the goal was the same—clarity. And both ways seemed to involve a period of confusion in the process.

All at once the front door burst open and a knot of people exploded into the room, shoving and giggling. They piled inside until several of them saw Larry and suddenly sobered up, like drunks spying a policeman. The others followed suit and in a few moments the nine boys and girls became men and women, all of them in their thirties and forties. They arranged themselves in a ragged semicircle and stood awkwardly looking at Larry and Eleanor.

"Hi," Eleanor said. "This is Larry, my husband." Larry smiled in their direction, but the expression died on his lips as he saw what seemed embarrassment on their faces. In that moment he was convinced, as irrational as such certainty was, that they knew all about him, that Eleanor had used him as "material" in their workshop, and that they were in on some secret in which he served as victim or scapegoat. It was an intense spasm of paranoia or acute perception, and Larry took another swallow of beer to cover his own embarrassment.

"Hello," one of the women said, walking forward. "I'm Helen." She half-turned toward the others. "And that's Ralph, Frank, Jean, Margaret, Angie, Ed, and Roger."

Larry glanced sharply at the man at the end of the

group, remembering that he was the one who supposedly told Eleanor to take her locket off. In the flesh he looked nothing like either of the men in Larry's fantasies. He was middle-aged and paunchy, his face flaccid and his eyes shifty.

"Hello," Larry said, "I'll try to remember all the names." He turned to Eleanor. "I thought there were fifteen in the class."

"Not everybody comes every day," she replied.

The others unbent a bit and moved into the room, some of them taking seats on the pillows and several of them lying down and closing their eyes. No one said anything else. Larry realized that his presence was being registered and integrated. He took a deep breath and straightened his spine.

"Are we doing something?" The voice was Alec's and everyone turned in the direction it came from. The director was standing at the door to the kitchen, a look of exasperation on his face. "I hope we're doing something," he continued. "Waiting room, maybe. Or funeral parlor. Otherwise it would be too much like a bunch of dimwits hanging around my living room, wouldn't it?"

The tone of his voice was sharp and the others responded as though he had lashed them. The ones lying down sat up and the ones sitting brought some focus to their eyes. Larry watched as Alec prowled the room like a trainer in a cage full of tigers. He was glad of the man's presence if for no other reason than it seemed to take the heat off him.

But the grace period was very brief. Alec turned to

him. "Please excuse this," he said, "But this gang of *actors*"—he delivered the word with scorn—"Has a tendency to forget our purpose in being here. Send them out into the woods for an hour and they regress."

"Maybe I should leave," Larry said. "I don't want to get in the way of your work."

"Not at all," Alec boomed. "This is a rare treat for our little group. How often do we have an exalted zen master joining in our childish revels?"

"I'm not a zen master," Larry said defensively, feeling the sudden shift in direction of Alec's attack, "I'm only a student."

"Just what a zen master would say," Alec replied triumphantly. He swept the others with his glance. "However our guest defines himself, you must stay with your own role. His presence should sharpen your practice, not distract you from it." He turned to Larry again, his manner ingratiating. "In any case, I am going to prepare tea."

Alec spun around and retreated to the kitchen. Larry watched him leave and continued staring at the door after he'd gone. He wasn't quite sure how to behave. In part he felt he was being mocked. At the same time he was intrigued by the way Alec kept the mood of the group on edge. The man was obviously totally dedicated to his work, and a consummate professional. With a few deft strokes he'd drawn Larry into the spirit of the workshop.

Larry returned his attention to the group. Everyone was now sitting on a pillow, a conscious circle observing itself. No one spoke, but a great deal of communication was going on through the eyes. They all looked at one another, either glancing from face to face, or locking stares and holding them. Larry couldn't help but get involved, and he found himself gazing into the eyes of the woman who'd introduced herself as Helen. She was a petite woman with pepper and salt hair, and wearing the almost ubiquitous jeans and t-shirt. Like all the woman there, she did without a bra and he couldn't keep himself from looking at her breasts. To his surprise, when she saw him do that, she raised her chest slightly, as though offering her nipples to him. It was so subtle he almost wasn't sure she'd done that, but then she smiled at him in a way that left no doubt. She was flirting boldly, using a minimum of clues.

"Maybe her inner role is seductress," he thought. "She wouldn't be acting that way with Eleanor in the room if it wasn't some kind of exercise." The insight calmed him, but raised the question of how he should respond. Under ordinary circumstances, as a faithful husband and temporarily celibate zen student, he should accept any erotic offer with equanimity and compassion, treating it as the other person's projection. But here he was free to don any cap he wanted, and he began to see the edge that Alec was working with, the almost imperceptible line between illusion and reality.

Finally, he broke off the contact and looked to see what the others were doing. Their expressions varied, ranging from anger and suspicion to complicity and glee. Except for the man called Roger, whose face was flushed with lust. Larry followed his line of sight to the place he was fixed on, and saw that it was Eleanor he was coupled with. His stomach tightened. She was gazing back at the man with open desire. Her legs were spread apart, her feet flat on the floor and knees raised and falling to either side, her crotch exposed and seeming to pulse with energy. Larry blinked. For a few moments he thought this was another hallucination, an imposition of *makyo* on the palpable reality around him. But he was wide awake and seeing clearly, and Eleanor was radiating raw sexuality. He knew it had to be an exercise, that she wouldn't openly flaunt an actual affair she was having with Roger in this way, but the rational conviction could not compete with the flame beginning to burn in his belly.

"I can't leave you people alone for a minute!" Alec bustled into the room carrying a large tray with a teapot and a dozen cups. "This looks like a consciousness raising group for deaf mutes," he went on as he lowered himself to the floor and put the tray down in front of him. "The only real tension was the avoidance between Ralph and Jean. Eleanor and Roger's crude version of desire is something that should be saved for Broadway, as was Larry's imitation of jealousy. We can excuse him because he's an enlightened man merely amusing himself for an afternoon, but you characters are supposed to be working."

Alec's intrusion snapped the spell and everyone visibly relaxed. Eleanor pulled her antennae back in and discarded her aura of wantonness as efficiently as wiping lipstick from her mouth. And Roger turned back into his ordinary lackluster self.

Alec lined up the cups and poured tea, and when everyone had been served and were all sipping contentedly, Alec continued his criticism. "Life's a stage, remember? There are many sets, many costumes, many roles. But there is one difference from what we usually call theatre. In life there is no audience. You have to be the thing, not indicate it for someone else to pick up on. If someone else can read what you're doing and play back, that's great. But that has to happen spontaneously. You can't act for anyone else's benefit, not even your own. Any questions?"

"How do you know if someone is reading you correctly?" asked Helen. "I was feeling a rush of breath when I looked at Larry and he took it as a sexual signal, at which point I started feeling sexy, and then wondered whether that wasn't what was going on in me all along."

"That's always what's going on in you all along," Margaret put in, and everyone laughed.

"Well," Alec said after a few moments, "That's what you're supposed to be finding out. Choosing an inner role is not a mechanical exercise. The role changes even as you define it and use it. You've got to go through many changes before the essence becomes clear. With Larry, you were probably responding to his external role as a Buddhist figure, and then picked up the sexual vibrations he was giving off as jealous husband.".

"Were you really jealous?" Eleanor asked.

"Around here, who knows what's real?" Larry replied good naturedly.

"Isn't there a saying in zen," Alec interjected, "To the effect that when you attain realization you know it as sharply as you know the difference between hot and cold water?"

"Yes."

Alec swiveled his head to gather the attention of the others. "Well, that's how it should be with your inner role. Then, no matter what happens inside or outside, you aren't shaken or thrown off balance."

Something clicked in Larry's mind. "But that's like being crazy, isn't it? I mean, it's like having a private room in your mind that no one else can get into, and then there's a wall between you and everyone else."

"Exactly," Alec replied. "But this exercise doesn't create the wall. That's always already there. This work makes you aware of it. Not the ordinary defenses and partitions in the mind, but the basic wall of separation. The thing that defines you as 'I'. And when you have come to terms with that, then you can use it consciously or dissolve it. The first produces art, the second produces religion." Alec poured himself more tea. "Of course," he added, "You can fall between two stools, as Gurdjieff put it, and then the result will be madness. But then it's an open madness, not the conventional insanity that the world calls civilization."

"Maybe it would be better to leave it alone in the first place," Larry said.

"Maybe," Alec replied. "But you've made the leap with your commitment to zen. And you're finding yourself up against that wall, aren't you?"

With Alec's words, Larry remembered a time he'd gone to sit in a zendo run by a different school than his, where everyone sat facing a wall instead of open space. He recalled the feeling that if he sat long enough the wall would distintegrate, dissolve before his eyes. And suddenly he was very glad he'd come to the workshop, to discover that Eleanor was working on the same problem he was, from an entirely different method and tradition.

But no sooner had he reached that resolution than Alec once again yanked the rug out from under him. "For all you know," the director went on, "Eleanor may actually be having an affair with Roger and their exercise was a sophisticated kind of camouflage, a purloined letter before your very eyes. That would be a wall that would mock any insight you think you've attained, wouldn't it?"

As he had earlier, when Alec had nailed him as lying when he told Eleanor he'd dropped by on a whim, Larry got a sense of how dangerous the edges were in the workshop. Alec's game was like zen in another way, that whenever it seemed there had been a breakthrough, it proved to be an escape into another chamber of the prison. In zen, only final enlightenment got one outside, and Larry wondered what the equivalent was in Alec's system.

"What about you?" Larry asked Alec, "Are you free of all the walls?"

"My wife left me a long time ago," he replied.

There was something in Alec's voice, a sadness that wasn't self-pitying, that touched Larry at the core, even as he struggled to remind himself that even intonations of sincerity were not necessarily anything more than tools of interaction for Alec. Larry glanced at the others to see how they responded to his words, and found that they were all looking down or off to one side. Except for Eleanor. She was looking at him fiercely, with an expression he could not label.

It was more than he could handle. "Well," he said, forcing himself to smile, "It's been fascinating." He stood up. "Thanks for the tea and the exercise." He walked over to Eleanor, bent down and kissed her lightly on the lips. "See you later," he said.

"See you later," she replied.

"Thanks for dropping by," Alec said. "It was valuable for us too."

The others said their goodbyes and Larry went outside. More than anything in the world, at that moment, he didn't want to think or to feel. He got on his motorcycle and headed back toward his house, and the meditation room that had once seemed a port in the storm of life, but now appeared more like the eye of a hurricane.

— 8 —

He spent the afternoon sitting, with the usual result. By the time Eleanor returned he felt stable,
capable. She came back in a subdued mood, greeted
him pleasantly, took a shower, and made dinner. The
meal was a bit strained. They had to talk about the
afternoon, but neither of them wanted to bring up
any details that might lead to hostilities, so they kept
the conversation general. Larry talked about the par-
allels he found between Alec's work and zen practice.
Eleanor told stories about some of the experiments
Alec had tried with them. From the outside, they
would have seemed to be having an amiable evening,
and on one level they were; but between them there
was a map of the mine field that they had to negotiate
in order to maintain any communication at all.

After dinner Larry did the dishes and Eleanor went
into the living room. When he joined her he found
that she'd built a fire and was sitting in the easy chair
reading.

"Interested in t.v. tonight?" he asked.

"No, I'd rather get into this. Alec asked us all to
read it. But you go ahead if you want, I can go into
my room."

At the mention of her bedroom, Larry flinched inwardly, remembering how he'd gone through her clothing and searched the dresser and found the cigarettes and Polaroid. "No," he said, "I'm going to try to finish *Letting Go*."

"That's the one you said was so hard to read."

"It's like walking through wet cement."

Larry stretched out on the couch and picked up his book, and the two of them read for over an hour in comfortable silence, broken only by the crackle and occasional spit of the fire. Once Eleanor got up to stir the flame and throw on a few more logs, and when she moved again it was to ask Larry if he wanted tea.

"Love some," he said without looking up.

She came back a few minutes later holding a tray with a teapot and two cups. He sat up and, instead of going back to her chair, Eleanor sat on the couch next to him. She was wearing the white kaftan she usually put on in the evenings and the fabric was a pallette of red and orange reflections from the fire. As she poured the tea her face was calm, inscrutable, and he was taken with the feeling that he didn't know her at all. She was familiar, but mysterious.

"How're you feeling?" he asked.

"Tired, I guess. And lonely."

"Lonely?"

"It's been such a long time since you've held me. I don't mean for sex, I mean just holding me." Her expression remained the same and there was no movement in her body, but tears welled from her eyes and rolled down her cheeks.

Larry was aghast. He had no sense now that she was

acting, but only felt the sadness that emanated from her. In a flash, all of his suspicions, all of the distancing he'd done, struck him as cruel, a selfish scrambling for survival at the expense of his caring for Eleanor. He reached out and took her hands in his. "I . . ." he began, but she shook her head. "Please," she said, "No words. I just need you to hold me."

He put his arms around her but their position was awkward and he slowly fell back on the couch, bringing her with him. They straightened their legs and shifted around until they fit perfectly, embracing one another, pressing their bodies together, faces cheek to cheek. Larry felt the wetness of her tears against his skin and he held her more tightly. She caught her breath, convulsed once, and then began sobbing, gently and almost soundlessly.

They lay like that for a long time, until Eleanor became still. He pulled back a few inches and kissed her eyes and wiped the moisture from her face. She blinked once and looked at him. "I'm sorry for breaking down like this," she said. "But I just felt lost."

Larry smiled. "I guess this is our week for having good cries."

"Our week," she repeated. "It seems forever since we talked about anything that was ours instead of yours and mine."

"Well, we've been pursuing different paths."

"Are we going to make it, Larry? Are we still going to be together in September?"

"Maybe. There are times when it doesn't look like it, but maybe our bond is stronger than we are."

"Boy, you sure can be romantic," she said, teasing.

"It's hard to talk mush when you've got a shaved head," he replied.

She nuzzled against him. "Can we just lie here for a while? It feels so good."

"Best idea I've heard all day."

They squirmed about until they were as close as they could get, as much of their bodies touching as possible, and when they were comfortably glued together they didn't move at all, but sank slowly into the soft cushions of the couch, the pull of gravity, and the breath rising and falling between them, until it seemed they were a single organism and could not distinguish where one left off and the other began.

Larry felt himself dozing, and was startled when Eleanor turned sharply, rolling first to her back and then to her other side, but he settled back into somnolence when she pressed herself against him again, wriggling a bit until concave and convex matched, her spine curved into his chest and belly, her buttocks in the hollow between his hips, knees aligned, and his toes sliding against the soles of her feet.

Her head rested on his left arm, and he put his right arm around her. But as he did so, his hand came to rest on her breasts. He felt a moment's hesitation, then cupped one breast in his palm, squeezed gently, and relaxed his fingers. The touch was one of sensuous reassurance, but not without its erotic undercurrent. At the same time, there was a familiar warmth and tingling beginning in his thighs and belly, and finally a stirring of his penis as it nestled close to the promise between Eleanor's thighs.

For a few moments he wondered whether he should go with these promptings, but decided against it. Both of them had been rubbed raw recently and while sex would certainly feel good it might open up wounds that should be allowed to heal. The important thing, he reasoned, was that they remain affectionate and test the foundations of their life together. Given that, sex would flower in its proper time.

He took several deep breaths, his stomach ballooning against Eleanor's back, and shortly he began to drift toward sleep again. Eleanor was very still and he guessed she was already out. The fire burned down and the tea grew cold in its cups. "Maybe we'll just sleep here like this tonight," Larry thought as his consciousness shut down. "I'll have to get a blanket sometime during the night."

That was the last thing he remembered before being awakened by a sound he didn't recognize at first, and then located as coming from Eleanor. She was making noises in her sleep, obviously having a dream. At first there were whimpers, like those of a child who's lost its mother in a crowd. Then, as Larry became more alert, they changed into moans and gasps. He thought they were sounds of fear and that she was having a nightmare, but in a moment realized he was at the wrong end of the spectrum. Eleanor had begun to move her pelvis and was grinding against him. And with that, the sounds she was making lost all abiguity and he recognized the unequivocal cadences of mounting desire.

Larry smiled in the dark, feeling privileged and

protective, but his expression froze on his lips when Eleanor cried out softly, "Oh yes, Michael, oh yes." His body went stiff, as though someone had slid a long, thin, icy needle into the base of his spine.

"Hold on," he told himself. "It's just a dream. And maybe you didn't hear right. Don't start getting crazy again."

But his advice was shredded both by Eleanor's increasing frenzy and the erection that was rising of its own accord and rushing to meet the invitation of Eleanor's churning buttocks. Then she whispered, "Michael," once more, so distinctly that he could have no doubt about what he was hearing. Larry continued to lie there and hold her, but felt like a man who has just been pushed from a cliff. There was nothing he could do but wait until he hit bottom.

After a while, Eleanor stopped moving and talking. She smacked her lips several times, and then became completely still and silent. Larry waited a few minutes and, as delicately as he could, disentangled himself and slipped off the couch. When he stood up he was fiercely awake, burning with emotion. He wanted to shake Eleanor and question her, but realized how pointless and harsh that would be. Their lying together had revived feelings of closeness he'd put on the shelf, and having them not only yanked away but turned against him left him stunned and hurt.

"Maybe it's nothing," he said to himself, "But why am I trembling?" And, with an almost audible click in his brain, like that of a radio being switched on, the competing voices started their dialogue in his mind.

"What do you need," one said, "Handwriting on the wall? She's got another man, maybe more than one."

"You're off the deep end again," said a second voice. "She was having a dream. How many times have you dreamed about old girlfriends? How do you know what you've said in your sleep?"

"It isn't just that," replied the first voice. "What about the torn panties, and the night she came home late, and the bruise on her throat?"

"You call that evidence of something?" came the rejoinder. "None of that proves anything. It's just your imagination seeing patterns where there are none."

And as though on cue, the third voice cut in. "Why are you caught in this struggle at all?" it said. "This is all *maya*. There's nothing here but a woman asleep on a couch. Let her be whatever she is. Don't get involved in her actions and feelings. The true teaching is dispassion and universal friendliness. Stay away from intensity and entanglements."

"I can't just run away," Larry said to himself, blanking out the voices. "She isn't just a body lying there, and she isn't only my wife. She is the focus of all my meditation, the *koan* that life has given me. Loving her or hating her is not enough. I have to *solve* her."

He turned and left the room silently. He went into his bedroom and put on a sweater and socks and a woolen cap, then went outside and into the woodshed. The night was cold but he knew from experience that after a half hour of sitting he wouldn't feel the temperature. He lit a candle and a stick of incense, and lowered himself onto his pillow. He assumed the posture and with a great act of will hurled himself into his sitting, like a sweating man might dive into a cool lake.

He sat until dawn, moving only to light a second candle when the first burned out, and to put a new stick of incense in the holder from time to time. The woods all around were uncannily quiet, and all the houses for miles around were dark. Larry felt as though he were the only person awake in the world.

It took over an hour for his feelings to subside and his mind to empty, and then the magic took over once again, with all human complexity seen from a distance as a bizarre frenetic melodrama, and only the simple structure of the body itself and its ancient rhythms of heartbeat and circulation and breath as real. By the time the sun appeared, Larry had regained his center.

He got up and went into the bathroom to pee and wash his face, and then returned for the regular two sessions he ordinarily sat each morning. He realized that nothing had been resolved as far as his uncertainty about Eleanor's fidelity, but the entire problem had been put in perspective. And as he listened to the first birdsongs and watched the space get brighter with the day, he was sure he would see the matter through with the compassion and dignity that had become his ideals.

But his composure was rattled by the sound of the car starting up and moving off down the road. It wasn't yet seven o'clock and Eleanor had never left so early before. He frowned but did not move until the timer went off, indicating that the forty-five minutes was up. Then he stood, bowed, blew out the candle, and went into the house.

As he walked to the front door he noticed that the sky was grey and the rising sun had already disappeared behind a thick cloud cover. Rain seemed certain. He went into the kitchen and saw that Eleanor had not made coffee, and there was a note slipped under the napkin holder on the table.

"I'm sorry," it read, "But I just couldn't deal with my feelings this morning. I was afraid that if we had breakfast together I'd say things I'd regret later. I woke up in the middle of the night and found that you were gone. I was shivering with cold and wondered why you didn't at least put a blanket over me if you were going to leave me there. I went to the woodshed and peeked in and found you sitting on your pillow in the dark. It was too weird. The shaved head, the robe, staring at a statue, looking like a zombie. And not caring that we'd been holding each other. I still love you but I don't know how much more of this I can handle." It was signed, "E."

Larry flexed his brain to keep his mind empty. He refused to be drawn into Eleanor's reactions. The only part of her note that nicked his conscience was her reference to his not putting a blanket over her. That was definitely a lapse in common consideration, but then so was her calling out another man's name in her sleep. As to the rest, however weird she found his appearance in the meditation room, it was no stranger than the antics that went on in Alec's class.

"Where did she go at this hour?" he wondered. "To

have coffee in town, or else to see her lover?" He waited for the fantasies that seized him when he began to think about Eleanor and another man, but this time there was nothing. He even tried to conjure an image, but found he couldn't even picture Eleanor's face much less what expressions she might produce making love to someone else. He felt relieved at first and then apprehensive. As disturbing as the erotic fantasies had been, at least he'd still felt a connection to her. Now, it was as though she'd been erased, or had erected some psychic shield so he couldn't even find her in his mind.

"Maybe it's really over between us," he thought, and with the idea felt a great loss and liberation. Without her there would be an imbalance for a while, a sense of having had a leg cut off. But then he would enter a new space, one in which he did not have to be concerned with her wants and needs, or have to modify his own course of action to coincide with her studies and career.

In any case, she was gone for the day, and he had to look after his own schedule. He made tea and ate breakfast, then shaved and showered, the hot water taking the stiffness of the all-night sit out of his muscles, and by the time he was in the living room, enjoying a second cup of tea and a cigarette, the day had begun to darken, promising not only rain but a storm.

— 9 —

The storm seized the earth and sky in its passionate embrace. Larry leaned against the thick trunk of a pine tree, his arms curved behind him to hug the rough bark. He was barefoot, and naked under the long slicker that covered him from ankles to head.

The air was water, for the rain had assumed command of the night and brought the other elements under its sway. The ground had turned to mud. Only the lightning vied for supremacy, exploding sporadically. Otherwise, there was only blackness, a thick dimensional blackness that went on into eternity, the mysterious emptiness in which the galaxies swam. But when the lightning did flash, creation occured, and the woods was etched in brilliant detail for a jagged fraction of a second. Trees and shrubs and startled deer lept from nothingness into being, held for an instant, poised, motionless, real beyond all imagining, and then lapsed back into primordial darkness.

Larry shivered with a chill that had nothing to do with cold. The tremors bubbled up his spine and broke in his brain where such a tumult of sensuous realization cascaded through his mind that his face

flew apart and he laughed wildly into the incessant
clatter, roaring at the thunder.

It was almost midnight, and Eleanor had not yet
returned. Waiting for her had pushed him over the
edge of any pretense at self-control and he'd run into
the forest to find a force to balance his wildness. He'd
been there for an hour by the clock but had swung
into a space that contained no measures for mechanical time. He had shouted and screamed his way into
a primal animality, and looked and acted like one of
the classic zen crazies who appear in Buddhist paintings.

The entire day's sitting had been focussed on Eleanor. He installed her in his awareness the way another student might use *mu,* or any of the traditional
koans. He breathed her and envisioned her, felt her in
the straightness of his spine and the immobility of his
legs. He didn't indulge in any thoughts of her, but
simply incorporated her as a presence in his being.

By dinnertime, when he got up from his final session, a decision stood up with him. He was ready to
confront Eleanor about her note and to engage if
necessary in a knock-down battle until they got clear
about how they really felt about continuing their marriage. Waiting until September now seemed arbitrary.
If it indeed was over between them, it would be best
to settle that at once.

But she didn't return. By seven he was annoyed, by
eight worried, and by nine angry. "I can't believe she's
pulling this number again," he said to himself. "And

that I'm going through exactly the same changes." By eleven he was beside himself. Eleanor had either had an accident or was purposely staying out. He doubted the former possibility for the police would certainly have been by. She was either punishing him or had decided to live with her lover after all.

It was then that the fantasies began again, more vivid than ever, fueled by a day of concentrating on her. Eleanor appeared on the screen in his mind lying naked on a rug in front of a fireplace, a man next to her. But this time the man's face and figure were blurred and hazy. They lay side by side, talking.

"Would you believe it?" she was saying. "He was holding me and I could tell he was aroused. He even put his hand on my breast. And then he nodded off. And when I woke up he was gone and didn't even have the decency to cover me with a blanket."

"And you found him in the woodshed?" the man replies.

"God, it was so spooky."

"The man is obviously sick," her lover says, solicitously. "He needs help."

"What should I do?"

"You've done it. You've left him. Maybe that will wake him up and he'll go see a shrink." The man puts one hand on Eleanor's belly and begins rubbing and kneading the flesh, spreading the arc of his caress until he moves from her nipples to her clitoris, stroking gently, pinching lightly. She sighs and squirms closer to him.

"You're sure it's the right thing?" she asks.

"Even if I didn't want you myself, if I were just a friend giving you advice, that's what I'd tell you."

She puts her head on his chest. "Oh Michael, I don't know what I'd have done without you. You're so strong."

When the Eleanor of his mind's eye had begun to kiss her phantom lover's body and started to go down on him, Larry lost his control. Outside the house the storm was peaking, lashing with unbridled fury at the ancient mountains in its path. He'd thrown off his robe and put on the full-length slicker and strode out into the wind and rain, and raged like Lear at the elements.

He might have stayed there for hours except, at midnight, he saw the lights of Eleanor's car making its way up the road, the high beams flipping through the trees like a stick held by a running child hitting the slats of a fence. Larry had traveled so far back into primal consciousness that for a few seconds he gazed at the lights as an aborigine might, simply not knowing what the contrivance was.

And then, in an instant, he returned to his conventional identity. Suddenly he was a deranged husband waiting for his wife to come home, and a student of zen discovering that his practice had pitfalls that had been described well enough in the abstract but never in relation to a situation such as his. He stood perfectly still for a minute, breathing deeply and composing himself, and then walked back to the house.

He opened the door and stepped inside just as Eleanor was going into her bedroom. She turned to face him. She looked very drunk and her mouth was puffy, almost bruised. She took one step forward, her hip jutting out. She exhuded a randy, raunchy recklessness. "Well, well," she drawled. "It's our little monk."

The taunt, the attitude of aggressive abandon, the seeming evidence of having been at least kissing a man for hours, were like claws across his chest. He took two steps forward, his knees shaking. It was clear to him in that moment that no amount of sitting, no number of zen teachings, could ever serve as ballast against the blasts of her emotional power. "Eleanor," he said, his voice thin.

She stared at him for a few seconds and then underwent a compelling transformation. Keeping the exterior aspect of the wanton wife, she seemed to drop back inside herself and collect herself around a different personality. It was as though her present character became transparent and he could see through it how she felt inside, and what he saw was a lost little girl. He couldn't tell whether he was hallucinating, or observing the inner role that Alec had talked about, or was just a man seeing that the woman who was his wife was many women.

"Larry," she said, her eyes filling with pain, her lips quivering.

As he looked at her changes, he felt what little sense of his own identity he still had dissolving even further. So much of who he felt himself to be had become dependent on his relationship to her that she could now literally throw him into confusion simply by altering the shape of the mirror she held before him. And now he had lost all context for knowing her, this Eleanor, this woman, this living *koan*.

"Eleanor," he repeated and took another step forward. But even as he moved she changed again. She became all hard glittering surfaces, impermeable. Her mouth turned into the slit of a gun turret, her eyes the barrels of a cannon. It was Pirate Jenny on the steps of the hotel, and every man inside would be dead in a few minutes.

"No," she said, "It's too late. You waited too long."

He raised a hand toward her, but she spun around quickly and stepped into her room. She turned one last time and her face was now a mask of sorrow, tears rolling down her cheeks. "I loved you so much," she said, and then slammed the door shut. He heard the inside bolt slamming into place.

He stood there staring stupidly at the door. He pushed back the hood of the slicker and ran one hand over his scalp. He realized that there was a small puddle at his feet where the rainwater had dripped onto the floor. He was stunned, and reached for whatever would bring some sense of normality back into the moment. He decided to make some tea.

But as he walked toward the kitchen he noticed Eleanor's handbag lying on the table next to the couch, still wet from her short trip from the car to the house. It was lying on one side, as though she'd casually tossed it down when she came in, and some of the contents had spilled out. One item was unfamiliar, and he went over to look at it more closely. It was a flat, round, plastic case, and when he picked it up he remembered what it was, the holder for Eleanor's diaphragm, something she hadn't used for several years since she switched to the pill, which she was slightly afraid of but felt would allow more aesthetic lovemaking. He remembered that when they'd agreed on a summer of celibacy, she'd expressed relief at not having to take the pill for three months.

He opened the case. The rubber shield was there. It was warm. And it was covered with secretions and spermicidal cream. He sat down heavily on the couch. His lips trembled. And his first hot tears fell onto the coated surface forming tiny droplets.

"I can't handle this," he said out loud and lept up and walked rapidly into his bedroom where he took off the slicker, put on pants, shirt and boots, scooped up some money, threw the raincoat back on, and went outside once more, this time to jump on the motorcycle and roar off into the night.

If he'd paused even for a second he wouldn't have attempted the trip, riding down a mountain road during a violent storm. But he was more driven than driving, and the grace which is said to protect madmen and drunks kept him from the accident the circumstances would have predicted. He rode blindly, drawing stares of astonishment and concern from people going by in cars who felt it was risky enough negotiating those roads with four wheels and a roof over one's head.

He drove to the Joyous Lake, a large restaurant and bar that took its name from one of the chapters in the *I Ching*, and which served as a club house for the locals and the major entertainment center for the summer people. There was music every night, mostly provided by a band of four or five of whichever musicians happened to be around that evening.

On the night Larry went in, the storm had kept the audience to a very small crowd, and when Larry entered he caused a stir. Water was pouring off his slicker and with the hood back his bald head shone red in the cabaret lighting. His eyes were blazing like Fourth of July sparklers.

The regulars, used over the years to a long progression of eccentric millionaries, legendary dealers and home-grown hermits, were rarely stirred to interest by any idiosyncrasy of dress or manner. But Larry impressed them.

"What's he on?" said a heavy-set man with a bushy golden beard.

"I don't know," said his companion, a man that could have been the twin of the first except that his hair was black. "But that's about as crazy as I've ever seen."

To Larry, the space was a jumble of sound and color, an impressionist refuge from the sharp contours of his life. He went to the bar and ordered a beer, and as he did thought of Alec's getting him to have a drink the day before, and wished the man were there to talk to. As it was, the other people in the place might have been from Pluto. He felt very alone, and got up to go over to the cigarette machine.

"Do you think he's for real?" said a lanky brunette to her girlfriend.

"He looks like he's just swallowed a couple of thousand mikes of acid," said the second woman.

Larry went back to the bar, tossed off the first beer, ordered a second, and lit a cigarette. He sat and smoked for several minutes and felt himself calming down. Slowly, his flashing jagged aura became smoother and dimmer. His breathing returned. And by the time the band had finished its set and Larry was on his third beer and second cigarette, he had become inconspicuous, just a bald man in a raincoat sitting at the bar.

His heart was sore and his brain a traffic jam of conflicting thoughts. He was also beginning to feel the slight delirium that comes from lack of sleep. He'd already stayed up through one night and was well into his second, and fatigue ate away at whatever little balance and stability he had at that moment.

"What should I do?" he wondered. "Go back and kick the door in and wave the diaphragm in Eleanor's face? Not go back at all? What do I want?" The last question was the easiest to answer. What he wanted was peace, the peace that he found in sitting. But now that it seemed he'd lost her, he also yearned for Eleanor. Not as she was now, not as they'd become, but as the dream of union they'd shared early in their marriage. "Is it possible?" he wondered, "After all this? And would it be foolish to try? Maybe it's best to just let it lie, suffer all of this now instead of running the risk of causing even more pain and damage by attempting a reconciliation." A sharp pain shot through his chest as he asked himself whether he would ever be able to make love with Eleanor again knowing she'd been with another man.

Larry sat there for over an hour, looking more and more like any troubled man drowning his problems in drink and introspection. And when his emotions had settled, his mind took control once more, and its directive was clear. Larry realized he couldn't just let Eleanor slip away, nor could he walk out on the marriage without confronting her. If that happened, he saw, he'd always be tormented by a sense of failure, of not having solved the *koan*. If there was to be a break between them, it had to be clean, mutual, and out in the open. He decided to go back and force the issue.

When he went outside, the storm had ended. The night was soft, subdued, and his drive back to the house was slow and easy, almost a meander through the sweet rain-washed air. He felt focussed, resolved. He would face Eleanor and know once and for all whether they could fit into one another's lives.

He pulled into the driveway and it wasn't until he'd dismounted and taken several steps that he realized that the car was gone. He looked around sharply. All the lights in the house were on. He froze for an instant and then he was running, flinging open the front door and charging inside. The door to Eleanor's room was open. He stepped inside.

She was gone.

The bureau drawers were open and empty, the closet vacant, the suitcases missing. Her vanity table had also been cleaned out. On the pillow of her bed Eleanor had placed a letter. It took him a few seconds before he was able to move, and then he walked over and picked it up.

"You," it said at the top. And then continued underneath, "I was going to write Dear Larry but I realized how dreadful that would sound. This is not easy for me, but I didn't want to leave without some kind of goodbye.

"We once spent an afternoon lying in bed in our apartment. We held each other for hours and you said to me, You are my true home. Not this apartment or this city or anywhere in the world, except where you are.

"I know that that's the kind of stuff that gets written off as romantic, but I know you meant it and how you meant it, because I felt the same way.

"After we got married we had the usual problems, but none of that mattered so long as we were home for one another. Not even if I spent most of my time in the theatre and you went off to your meditations. I never wanted to keep you from anything, so long as when you came back you were coming back to me.

"Now it doesn't feel like that. Zen isn't something you do when you're not with me, it's become a substitute for me. And maybe I'm to blame, maybe we should have had children, maybe I shouldn't have stayed so wrapped up in acting. But I never lost sight of you, and I think you don't know me anymore.

"I hope you find what you're looking for. I know I have. I want a man who can be his own man and still have room for me in his heart and mind. I don't want to be married to a monk."

The note wasn't signed.

Larry stood without moving for a long time. He held the letter tightly in his hands, his head thrown back as though he'd been struck a blow on the neck. The room smelled of Eleanor's perfume. Her absence was palpable.

He shook himself and walked back into the living room. "Well, you're free now," he thought, "You can go sit as much as you want."

He went into his room, took off the slicker, and put on a sweater. He walked outside and into the wood-shed. The sky was clearing and the moon brightened the path and the inside of his meditation chamber. He looked at the space that symbolized and embodied the way of life he'd chosen, and for which he'd risked, and lost, what had been most precious to him.

But it was all changed now. He saw it as Eleanor must have, a bizarre artifact, a place for an absurd ritual. It seemed alien, foreign, a cave of solitude for a lonely man. He stared at the pillow for a long time, his mind blank. And then in a single fluid motion he spun around, picked up the axe that was standing next to the door, swung it over his head, and brought it down on the raised board that served as an altar. It cracked, and the statue of Buddha, the incense holder and the candle went flying into the air. Then he attacked the pillow, but on the first blow the axe merely bounced off, and he swung again, this time splitting the cloth. His eyes glowing fiercely, he hit it again and again until it was cut to shreds, the cotton ticking inside spread over the entire floor. He didn't stop until the ache in his arms and shoulders made it impossible for him to lift the axe again.

He tossed the tool to the ground and leaned against a wall, panting. And when his heart and breath were no longer racing, his face formed into a mask of resolve. The crisis of doubt was at its climax, and the *koan* had permeated his entire being. The zen practice had brought him this far, but to take the next step he had to go beyond sitting or studying. He had to plunge into life.

— 10 —

He drove steadily. The moon was very bright now, its ghostly light caressing the ancient mountains and broad plains. It was almost three in the morning and Larry had the road to himself. He was possessed by a crazed lucidity that made his going to Alec's seem logical and even necessary. Rationally he knew that the director would probably not be able to help him find Eleanor, but Alec was the only link he had to her just then.

He sped past sleeping houses and roused dogs into barking. It was the end of the week and everyone else was resting after a normal day in which people had presumably managed their affairs without worrying about enlightenment or having their mates run out on them. In the morning there would be work to be done, children to be tended. It was the ordinary routine of humanity and Larry wondered if he would ever be part of anything like that again.

An old poem from one of his zen texts came to mind:

> Let us admire the moon and cherish the flowers—
> Thus we should like to live.

Never to try to become Buddha
And ruin our precious life!

Larry leaned into the wind whipping past as the bike splashed through puddles. "What will I do?" he asked himself. It seemed that his marriage was finished. His confrontation with Eleanor, whenever that happened, would probably only put the final period on their relationship, and that left him free to pursue his practice. But at that moment, he wasn't at all sure he would go back to it. He understood that his destroying the altar and pillow was an act of desperation and frustration, and yet it had a sense of closure.

Eleanor's leaving and his catharsis in the meditation room seemed to balance one another. And as he roared toward Mount Tremper through a landscape that might have appeared in a Japanese watercolor, he was overtaken by the realization that suddenly he was a free man. He felt a youthful liberation and abandon he'd not enjoyed since before he met Eleanor. "I know who I am," he thought, "Why the hell have I been shaving my head and sitting on my ass all this time?"

And when he saw the full equation, the insight was so startling that he jerked the handles of the motorcycle and almost skidded on the slippery asphalt. The marriage, he saw, had eaten not only his independence but his very sense of self. The early years of ecstatic union had absorbed both him and Eleanor into the dream of an eternal "we," and he had lost the clear focus of his own "I." And zen had been what his drowning self had grasped at in order to keep from being permanently submerged, and then itself become a threat to his individuality. But now that he was alone again, there would probably be no further need to wield the sword of Buddhism or submit to its rituals and scriptures.

"Maybe I'll just go back to the city and pick up where I left off," he told himself. He could see himself in New York again, running his store and getting in touch with old friends who would be glad he was letting his hair grow again. There would be the stickiness of a divorce to deal with, but if Eleanor was with another man, the apartment would be his. And there would be women again. Eventually, he might even remarry, this time a woman who wanted children instead of a career.

By the time he turned into Alec's driveway he was hoping that she might even be there, that she'd stopped at the director's house as a way station, and that he could settle things with her on the spot, and get a chance to say his own goodbye and not be left hanging with her note as the final word. But when he shut the engine and heard the echo of the roar that had just ceased reverberating through the silent woods, he became aware of just how irrational his going there was. It was the middle of the night and he'd probably wakened dozens of people with his ride. He got off the bike and found himself swaying, and then realized how tired he was. This was his second night without sleep, his wife had run off with another man, his zen practice had exploded out from under him, and he'd been driving a motorcycle up and down mountains in a blinding rain storm.

He was wondering whether he shouldn't return home and come back later in the day when Alec's voice came booming out of a window. "If this is anybody's idea of an acting exercise, they'd better be prepared for a punch in the nose. If it's anybody else, watch out for buckshot."

Larry cleared his throat. "It's Larry," he said.

There was a long silence, and Larry heard whispers. And then Alec's voice again. "Hang on, I'll be right out."

A minute passed and Alec opened the front door. He was barefoot, wearing sweat pants and a flannel shirt. His face was still rumpled from sleep but his eyes were alert.

"I'm sorry to wake you," Larry said.

"I'm sure there's a good reason," Alec replied.

"Eleanor's gone."

"Ah," Alec said.

"You don't seem surprised."

"I can't say that I am."

"Is she here?"

Alec raised his eyebrows. "Why should she be here?"

"I don't know. You're her friend. And I heard voices a minute ago."

"That's my lover. You want to meet him?"

A voice called out from the other room. "Is everything O.K.?" it asked. It was a man.

"Fine. Just some domestic trouble," Alec said loudly. "Go back to sleep, I'll take care of it."

"I didn't mean to intrude," Larry said.

"Well, you're here. I guess you'd like to talk. Come in, I'll make some coffee."

"You're sure it's all right?"

"I'm usually up at six anyway. A couple of hours won't make that much difference." Alec stepped back from the doorway and Larry walked in past him. Alec pushed the door shut behind him and led him through the living room and into the kitchen. He switched on the light and they stepped into a large room that was crammed with shelves and cabinets and hanging plants. In the center of the space stood a round oak table with six chairs around it.

"Have a seat," Alec said. Larry sat down and Alec went to the stove and turned on the flame under a tea kettle, and then carried cups and spoons to the table, got a pitcher of cream from the refrigerator and put it next to the sugar bowl. His movements were slow and measured, giving Larry a chance to come down a bit from the intensity of his ride.

"Do you know where she is?" Larry asked.

"I can't do two things at once," Alec replied. "Let me make the coffee and then we'll talk." He went to the counter next to the sink and measured out some coffee into a filter, then waited for the water to boil, and when the kettle was whistling he picked it up, held it for several seconds, and poured it into a Pyrex holder. Then he waited for the entire thing to drip through before bringing the pot to the table. During the whole ritual he stole glances at Larry who was sitting forward, elbows on the table, eyes closed, his head resting in his hands.

"Let's try some of this," Alec said as he poured the coffee into their cups. They each took sugar and cream, and after a sip Alec reached into his shirt pocket and pulled out a pack of Camels. "Like a cigarette?" he asked.

Taken off guard, Larry simultaneously reached for a cigarette and said, "No thanks, I don't smoke."

Alec looked at him quizzically as Larry put the cigarette in his mouth. "You're a funny man," he said. "With you even smoking is a riddle."

"Eleanor and I gave it up," Larry said, taking a light from Alec who then lit his own. "Except that I went back and didn't tell her. So I've been smoking on the sly." He took a sip of coffee. "Then I learned that Eleanor's been smoking on the sly too."

"Really?" Alec said. "I never saw her smoke."

"Maybe only her inner role smokes," Larry said.

Alec smiled. "Good," he said. "If you can make a joke you're not as bad off as you look."

"Do you know where she is?"

Alec puffed on his cigarette. "You know," he said, "One of the few bits of wisdom I've acquired in my life is not to get caught between warring husbands and wives."

"There's no war."

Alec raised an eyebrow. "You come riding here at

three in the morning looking for your wife and you tell me there's no war? If there was peace you'd be home in bed. With her."

At Alec's last words, Larry winced. Alec saw the reaction and put his hand on Larry's arm. "I'm sorry," he said. "I know you're upset, and I don't mind sitting with you. But I really don't want to get involved."

"Please," Larry said, "It's important."

"Why? If she's run off with someone, what do you want with her?"

"Then you do know about him."

Alec stared down at the table and bit his lower lip. "What I know won't be of much comfort to you right now."

"I'm not looking for comfort. I want to know the truth."

"I thought you were finding that with your zen thing."

"Maybe that's finished too."

"I see," Alec said. He poured himself more coffee and lit a second cigarette.

"Who is he?" Larry asked.

"Someone you don't want to mess with."

"What?"

"Well, he's a powerful man."

"A weight lifter?"

"More like . . . let's say a businessman."

"What are you trying to tell me?"

Alec puffed on his cigarette as he had before, using it as a tempo to pace his speech. "Look," he said, "Eleanor is my student and friend. And I feel more than a little responsible for what's happened. You've seen what we do in the workshop. I try to get people to see their lives as theatre, and to play with their scripts, to take chances. Some of that affected Eleanor more than I had counted on, and she took a leap that was scary even to me."

"What kind of businessman?" Larry insisted.

Alec shrugged. "It's not clear. In fact, you might say it's a bit shady."

"What's Eleanor doing with someone like that?"

"She met him about a year ago. He saw her when she did that off-Broadway thing. Went to the theatre five nights in a row. Sent her flowers each night." Alec squinted through the smoke. "She had an affair with him," he added.

"A year ago!" Larry exclaimed, his stomach tightening. He shook his head. "Christ, I've been blind."

"The affair only lasted a few weeks," Alec went on. "She dropped him. But recently he showed up again."

Larry let out the air he'd been holding in his lungs, the tension in his stomach moving to his chest and shoulders. His eyes were dull and unseeing of anything around him. All his attention was fixed on the image in his mind, Eleanor lying naked in the arms of another man.

"I'm sorry to have to be the one telling you this," Alec continued. "But you asked. And since she is gone, you might as well know the details."

Larry looked up sharply, the hopelessness in his eyes suddenly replaced by a manic gleam. "What does she see in him?"

"It's more a question of what she doesn't see in you any longer. She's complained to me more than once that you'd rather stare at a wall than look at her. This man is older. He's in his fifties. He pays attention to her, he's interested in her career."

"Sure," Larry said, the word saturated with bitterness.

"The man's got money and influence. He can make things happen in the theatre world."

"Is he some kind of gangster? What's his name?"

"I don't want to say any more," Alec said.

"Is he dangerous? Is Eleanor in any danger?"

Alec raised his cup and took a swallow of coffee without taking his eyes off Larry. "He's dangerous," he replied at last. "But Eleanor's not in any danger. From what she tells me, he's in love with her."

"And her? Is she in love with him?"

"Maybe."

"I can't believe that. I want to hear that from her own mouth. I've got to see her."

"I'd put that idea on the shelf for a while, if I were you. He wouldn't take kindly to your showing up."

"She's my wife!"

"And he's got people working for him who take people for rides."

Larry's hand shot out and grabbed Alec's shoulder. "Look," he said, "I don't care about this guy and his goons. I want to see Eleanor."

"For what?"

"To talk to her. If she doesn't want to be with me any more, O.K. But she has to look me in the eye and tell me that it's over and that she's with another man. And the kind of man she's with."

Alec lit another cigarette. "If you really want that . . ."

"You'll tell me where she is?"

"Maybe they went back to the city. But she could be at his house in Shokan."

"Shokan. That's near the reservoir. That's where she went that morning."

"She didn't come to class every day," Alec added.

"Those remarks you made when I came to the workshop. You were trying to tell me."

"I suppose. Eleanor was furious at me afterwards. But when I'm working I get high on the process, and I go closer to the edge than I would in a conventional situation."

"Where's the house? Do you know?"

"I know."

Larry stared at him, his eyes hard and glittering. Alec did not respond for a long while and then sighed. "If I tell you it's only because I'm pretty sure he's not there now. A few days ago she told me he was going to Miami for a week." He lit a third cigarette. "It's that huge white house halfway up the mountain that you see when you're driving across the road that cuts through the reservoir."

"That's a chateau," Larry said.

"I told you the man is powerful."

Larry stood up.

"You're not going now?"

"If he's not there, it sounds like the perfect time."

"But he might have one of his men there guarding the place." Alec stood up also. "Look, why not go home and get some rest? Then you can drive over tomorrow. If the place is being watched, it won't be so dangerous in the daytime."

"This isn't that kind of trip," Larry said, remembering that there was one unresolved factor in his life. He might have lost his marriage and might never sit on a zen pillow again, but Eleanor was still his *koan,* and the momentum of that was charging him, making it impossible to stop until he'd seen it through.

"Well, do you have some kind of protection?" Alec asked, and added, sarcastically, "I mean, beside that unholy fervor that's glowing in your eyes."

"I have a gun back at the house. Do you think I should take it?"

"At this point I just want to wash my hands of this whole mess," Alec replied.

Larry took a deep breath, the air whistling past his nostrils. "Thanks Alec," he said.

"For what? I shouldn't even have let you in tonight. That's all I need now is to have your death on my conscience."

"It's my decision," Larry said.

"Then go with God," Alec replied, took two steps forward and put his arms around Larry's back and hugged him tightly. "Be careful," he said.

Larry returned the hug and the two men disengaged. "I'll walk outside with you," Alec said.

They walked out into the darkness. Larry kicked

the bike into life, switched on the headlight, waved once, and drove off. Alec stood there watching the tailight twinkle among the trees and listening to the roar of the engine grow dimmer until the woods was silent once more.

— 11 —

As he rode back to his house Larry forced himself to keep from thinking about what he was doing, for the moment he thought at all, his brain seethed with images. Now that he had a description of Eleanor's lover, the erotic film that had started up in his imagination over the past few days took on the textures of reality. Knowing that this was not *makyo* made it too painful to endure. So he clamped a lid on his mind and steered his course automatically.

When he returned, the first hint of dawn was changing the mood of the sky. It had not begun to become light yet, but the darkness had softened. He walked into the house and when he entered the living room he stopped and stood still, the events of the night suddenly seeming grotesquely unreal. But it was not a fantasy. Eleanor was gone, and Alec had not only confirmed his suspicions but revealed that Eleanor's infidelity had begun at least a year ago. The house still held a sense of her presence and Larry looked down at the couch, unable to accept that she had been lying there in his arms just the night before.

"Lying and lying," he said to himself. His jaw tightened and he went into Eleanor's bedroom. A part of him realized how insane his plan was, but that faint spark of reason was barely visible next to the white hot glow of passion that energized his will, fueled by anger, jealousy and hurt, and tempered by a concern for her well-being that was now more a sense of duty than an active feeling. For an instant he pictured himself being gunned down before her eyes and Eleanor collapsing in sorrow and remorse. "Serve her right," he said out loud as he strode to the night table next to her bed.

He yanked the drawer open and froze as he stared down at the empty space. The gun was gone.

It took a long while for the shock to wear off, for the electricity to stop buzzing up and down his spine, and when it did Larry found himself filling with a calm that was of a different dimension than anything he'd every experienced on his zen pillow, a relaxation that went beyond the level of body and mind and into the realm of fate. The last defense had been removed and if he was to meet his destiny with Eleanor he would have to do it unarmed, naked, vulnerable. The twin paths of marriage and meditation had met at this single point where the until-death-do-us-part of the one and the beyond-life-and-death of the other were forcing him to an overwhelming question. He was free, and so had no guide for his actions except his own decisions and spontaneous movements.

Strangely, he remembered an old quiz show in which, each week, successful contestants were asked whether they were content with their winnings or

wished to return the following week to risk what they
had in order to try to double their prize. Larry realized that he could drop the whole affair on the spot,
pack his things, rent a car, and go back to the city and
let Eleanor work out her own problems. But he was
also in the grip of a powerful momentum. Six years of
marriage and two years of sitting and the thrust of his
lifelong search for real identity were meeting at this
juncture, and he felt certain that if he did not see it all
through he would never fully be at peace with himself.

"Well, let's go for it," he said out loud, turned on his
heel, walked purposefully out of the house, mounted
his bike, and took off into what might be the first day
of the rest of his life, or the last day of his life altogether.

He drove to the reservoir, got a fix on the house
from across the water, and then figured out what
roads he'd have to take off the main highway to reach
the place. It took another half hour before he was at
the base of a packed-dirt road that ran almost a mile,
all uphill, to the chateau. There he stopped, shut off
the engine, and rolled the bike behind some trees. He
lit a cigarette and sat down next to the machine to
consider his approach.

Eleanor's taking the gun had several possible explanations. She might be afraid for her own safety and
brought it along as an ace in the hole. Or she was
afraid Larry might follow her and removed it to keep
him from having it, either worried that he might be
crazed enough to use it on her, or to prevent him

from the foolishness of pulling it on a professional armed bodyguard. He had no way of knowing whether there was a guard there, and if so whether Eleanor had warned him that Larry might show up.

Dawn was changing to morning. The sun would not appear for a while, but its light now ruled the sky. Birds were clearing their throats and Larry could see stray cars, their headlights still on, moving on the highway that ran north and south through the valley below. He ground out his cigarette and stood up, realizing that it was pointless to make a plan when he didn't know precisely what he was walking into. It was too late to weigh pros and cons. This was a singular turning point in his life and he had to enter it cleanly, as a man seeking truth and not as a guerilla on a commando raid. He began walking.

He made no noise as he moved. His mind was still, his breath deep. With each step it seemed the day grew brighter and when he was at the beginning of the long curved driveway that led to the large house, the edge of the sun was visible over the mountains, and reflected in the still water of the reservoir. He stood for a few minutes, watching the sunrise and drinking in the beauty of the land. The air was so sharp and pure it made his eyes tingle.

He turned and continued on toward the house. When he was almost there he saw Eleanor's car parked in front of the garage, but the doors were closed so he couldn't tell whether any other cars were inside. He walked to the front door, paused a moment, squared his shoulders, and tried the knob. It turned easily and the massive door sung open on oiled hinges, smoothly and silently.

Larry stepped into a foyer that was the size of his own living room, and through it into a living room that was bigger than the entire house he and Eleanor had been staying in. It looked like it had been furnished by an interior decorator. Carpet and drapes and paintings were all color coordinated, and every lamp and ashtray had been put into place according to some geometric design.

He walked through the room, moving now with almost exagerrated caution. At the far end was a door that led to a more normal sized room that looked like a study, with a desk, several chairs, a small sofa and bookshelves. On one wall hung a framed color photograph and when Larry saw it his stomach tightened. It was a picture of Eleanor. She was standing in front of a birch tree wearing a very brief bikini, one that Larry had never seen before.

"Bitch," he said out loud before he could catch himself. Then, all at once, he didn't care whether he made any noise of not, whether there was an armed thug in the house. He strode out of the study and back through the living room and out the other side into a dining room that opened onto an enormous kitchen space, where he found what he was looking for, the stairs that led to the second storey.

He took the steps two at a time and was panting slightly when he reached the corridor that curved out to the right and left from the top of the stairway.

There he paused and listened, and his scalp crawled when he heard a sudden sound, the unmistakable scrape of a bureau drawer being slid into place.

He walked in the direction of the sound. It had come from an open doorway halfway down the hall. He kept going until he reached the space and, without hesitating, spun past the edge and into the room beyond.

Eleanor was there. She was standing next to the bed on which she'd piled two suitcases, now open. She wore an almost transparent white peignoir and was holding one hand to her lips, looking at her belongings, thinking about what to unpack next.

"Getting comfortable, I see," Larry said.

She spun around. "Larry!" she exclaimed, her eyes wide with fright. But even as she called his name and her face registered fear, he was again taken with the uncanny sense that she was acting, playing a role, and doing it badly. She glanced past him and he turned his head to see what she was looking at. But there was nothing there.

"Expecting someone?" he asked.

"You shouldn't be here," she said. "It's dangerous for you."

"Is one of Michael's henchmen in the house?"

"How do you know about that?" she asked, and then a flash of understanding shot through her eyes. "Alec told you."

Larry took several steps into the room and Eleanor edged away from him. "Alec told me a few things," he said, "But nothing I didn't already suspect. Except that the details and the time frame were a little juicier than I expected."

"Why did you come here then?"

"To get you out of this for a start."

"I've made my decision," she told him and moved back another foot toward the head of the bed.

"To make love to a killer? For what? Just to see your name up in lights?"

"That's right," she replied, her shock wearing off and a touch of anger in her voice. "I want my name up in lights. I'm tired of seeing people with half my talent become stars. And Michael's not a killer."

"I'm sure. He has people to do that for him."

Eleanor stepped back another foot and suddenly Larry saw where she was going. As she turned and reached for the drawer of the night table, he leaped forward and slammed against her just as her hand was reaching inside. She fell on the bed and he stuck his own hand inside and closed his fingers around the gun. He picked it up, stood for a moment feeling its weight and its implications. Then walked back to the door and closed it.

"Now if we have company I'll be prepared to greet him."

"There's no one else in the house," Eleanor said dully, sitting up on the edge of the bed.

"I'm supposed to believe that?" Larry asked sarcastically, checking the cylinder of the gun and finding that it was indeed loaded.

"Believe whatever you want. But I'm not leaving here."

"Yes you are. I'm taking you someplace where we can talk. And when I've had my say then you can do whatever you want."

"There's nothing to talk about."

"Then you'll listen," he said and found himself waving the gun as he talked. It was a gesture he'd seen in gangster movies and he was astonished at how natural it felt.

"Would you mind not pointing that thing in my direction."

"Why? You should be used to having guns around. And if you'd reached it first, you'd be pointing it at me, and probably calling for your bodyguard."

"I told you there's no one else here."

"Like you told me you'd be faithful to me? Tell me, how many others have there been before this one?"

Once again, Eleanor underwent one of her sudden changes. Her eyes grew dark and her chin trembled. All at once she seemed on the verge of tears. "I'm sorry, Larry," she said.

"Cut the act."

"It's not an act," she cried out and now the tears did start flowing, coursing down her cheeks. And for all that he was convinced that she was playing on his sympathy, trying to buy time to gain control of the situation, the sight of her crying slightly unnerved him. "I loved you," she went on. "Yes, I had a little fling with Michael last year. I slept with him twice.

And then I felt so bad about it I had to stop. I didn't tell you because I didn't want to hurt you and I knew I wouldn't be seeing him again."

"Until next time."

"I didn't plan on a next time. Until you starting having your own affair with your pillow."

"It's not the same thing."

She took a deep shuddering breath, and her breasts trembled under the gauzy fabric. For the first time since entering the room Larry realized how sexy she looked and his chest constricted at the thought that her beauty was now for another man. She caught the look in his eyes and wiped the tears from her face, and then stood up, the front of the peignoir swaying open briefly to show a flash of belly and thighs and the tangle of pubic hair.

"Get dressed," he said.

She stared at him boldly. "Most men would ask me to get undressed," she said.

"Don't fuck with me," he shouted.

"Why? What are you going to do, shoot me? Go ahead."

Larry felt his control slipping, and began to see how limited his options were. Short of using physical violence, he couldn't force Eleanor to go with him. And he still wasn't certain whether one of Michael's thugs was in the house. If he started twisting Eleanor's arm and the other man came into the room, Larry would not only be exposed but legally in the wrong for entering a private house, carrying a gun, and assaulting a woman. But the alternative was galling. To admit defeat and ride away with his tail between his legs was something that would haunt him for the rest of his life. He saw that there was no direction to go but forward, to up the ante.

"Maybe I will," he said. "I've certainly got just cause."

"You wouldn't enjoy jail, or what Michael would do to you when he caught you, which he would."

"No," Larry replied, his voice cold. "Because after you I'd blow my own brains out."

Eleanor's mouth twitched. "You're bluffing," she said, but her tone was uncertain.

"You want to push it to the edge?, he replied.

"You're really crazy," she whispered.

He smiled. "You know, I may very well be."

They gazed at one another for a long time, and then Eleanor shrugged her shoulders. "All right," she said. "Let's take it to the edge." And with that unbuttoned the top clasp to the peignoir, pulled it open, and let it slip to the floor. Then, with the index finger of her right hand, she pointed between her breasts. "Right there," she said, "If you're going to do it."

"What do I do now?" Larry wondered. The barrel of the gun was pointing toward Eleanor but not at her. In less than a second he could aim and pull the trigger and she would be dead. What terrified him was that the action had such a sense of rightness to it, even a theatrical gloss. Then he would have no choice but to kill himself.

"Maybe that would be my satori," he thought.

"What are you waiting for?" she asked. "You going to give me a blindfold and a cigarette?"

Larry smiled again. "Have a smoke if you like. I know about your stash."

"Just like yours," she countered.

"You knew about that?"

"Oh really," she exclaimed, "Did you think you were hiding it from me?"

"Obviously not as well as you hid some things from me."

"What did you do, go through my drawers?"

"I had cause."

She regarded him levelly. "Sure," she said, "If I'm going to be executed, I'd like to have a last cigarette." She attempted to inject some bravado into her voice, but it could not mask the undercurrent of fear that ran beneath it. She reached into one of the suitcases and pulled out a pack of Pall Mall and a book of matches. "Mind if I sit down?" she asked.

"Go ahead."

"You're supposed to say, 'But don't make any funny moves'," she added. Eleanor pushed both suitcases off the bed, sat down her back against the pillows piled against the wall, pulled out a cigarette and lit it. Larry moved to the outside wall and sat in a chair from which he could see Eleanor, look out the window, and keep the door covered. Then he shook a cigarette from his own pack and lit it.

"Just like old times, isn't it?" she said.

"Except that we're sitting in your lover's house."

"And you're holding a gun on me."

"That's in case we suddenly have company," he said, but even as he spoke he was taken by the certainty that the house was indeed empty. He had no grounds for the feeling, but it was as clear as the sun which was now a few degrees above the horizon. Something else also nagged at him, but he couldn't pin it down.

Eleanor took a puff of her cigarette, blew out smoke, crossed her legs at the ankles, and looked over at Larry. "I still can't figure why you came here. If I were you, I wouldn't ever want to see me again."

"You've got something of mine," he said.

"What?"

"I don't know. All I know is that I'm right on the brink of understanding something, something I've been trying to contact inside myself for as long as I can remember. And coming here has to do with that."

She raised one eyebrow, a hint of disdain in her expression. "I thought you were finding all your answers on your precious pillow."

"I destroyed the pillow."

Eleanor started, surprise on her face. "Destroyed it?"

"I thought that would please you. I chopped it to pieces with an axe."

"You can get another one," she said.

"I can get another wife too."

"What for?" she replied. "You didn't do so hot with the first one."

"There are women who aren't liars and cheats in the world," he shot back, anger in his voice.

"And there are men who don't go running into the woodshed to sit on their ass everytime life gets a little confusing," she said, matching his anger.

"Maybe I wouldn't have needed that if you'd had a baby and been a real wife instead of showing your ass off on the stage," he yelled.

"Just like that?" she yelled back. "Have a baby? And what if you were the one who had to stop meditating because you were pregnant and couldn't go to your hotshot zendo because you had to take care of a kid all the time?" She ground the cigarette out in the ashtray next to the bed. "And as far as showing my ass off is concerned, you had enough chances to see it but you preferred looking at a wall."

Larry was about to shout back but remembered where he was. His intuition that the house was empty was strong, but not infallible, and his having an argument with Eleanor just then wasn't wise. He put his own cigarette out and shifted the revolver back to this right hand. The sun was now shining right into the room. Larry shut his eyes for a moment. His fatigue was catching up with him again and he wanted to be out of there, he wanted to sleep and forget.

"Larry," Eleanor said softly. He looked over at her. She had turned toward him and raised one leg, the knee high, her foot flat on the bed, her nudity transformed into nakedness. Under any other circumstances and to any other man, her desireability would have been overwhelming, and even in his condition Larry couldn't help but be moved.

"Larry," she repeated.

"What?"

"Look at me."

"I am looking at you."

"See me."

"I am seeing you."

"Are you?"

He stared at her. She leaned forward, one breast resting against the thigh of her raised leg, her eyes moist.

"Don't you know why you risked your life to come here? Really?" she went on, her voice even more gentle.

Tiny alarm bells went off in his mind. He could feel himself being drawn toward her, into her. Instinctively, his hand tightened on the gun, now pointed off to the side.

"Don't you understand?" she said.

"What are you talking about?" he replied, but even as he spoke he knew what her next words were going to be.

"You came here because you love me."

"I never denied that."

"You've been denying it for a long time. You've been afraid of it."

Once more he felt a tightening in his chest. He roused himself and stood up. "What difference does it make now?" he said, surprised at the depth of bitterness he heard in his voice.

"All the difference in the world."

"You've got someone else now."

She shook her head and smiled like a teacher

fondly correcting a favorite pupil. "There's no one else," she said.

Larry blinked several times and then, incongruously, laughed. "And what is all this?" he exclaimed, waving the gun in a wide arc to indicate the room and the house. And when his hand had completed the circle, the gun was pointing at Eleanor again. "Are you telling me that I'm having a hallucination?" he went on, his voice now steady.

"No," she told him, her voice equally calm. "You're playing out a role, but you don't have the script yet."

"Look," he told her, his eyes narrowing. "If I pull this trigger we're both going to be sorry. Do us both a favor. Make it easy for me to get out of here. And then I'll leave you alone and you can do whatever you want."

"What I want is to be with you," she said. "That's all I've ever wanted."

"Stop the double-talk!"

"Larry, I love you."

"You're driving me crazier than I already am."

"Just like that great doubt you used to tell me about."

"What?"

She leaned back against the pillow again, but kept her leg raised, and the motion exposed her crotch. He glanced involuntarily to the spot between her thighs and saw the deep violet ridge of vaginal lips beneath the thatch of hair. To his astonishment, he felt a stirring in his groin.

"I told Alec about that," she went on. "And he

suggested an acting exercise for me, a way I might create a little doubt of my own."

His eyes widened and it seemed that the floor was tilting under him.

"It started with the torn panties in the laundry basket," she said. "I assume you saw those."

His mouth fell open.

Eleanor licked her lips. "And then there was that bit with the locket. And after that the hickey." She smiled to herself. "That was the hardest one."

"It was all a trick?" he gasped.

"I like to think of it as my greatest role," she replied.

"I don't believe you."

"No? What about the night I came home with my clothes all torn and dirty. What did you believe then? And when you found the Polaroid in my drawer or the photograph downstairs? And when you found the diaphragm next to my purse?" She ticked off each event relentlessly.

For a few moments he was swayed by what seemed like evidence that all his suspicions had been consciously planted by Eleanor, and then he remembered one item she'd left out. "And when we were lying on the couch, were you pretending to be asleep when you whispered those things?"

Larry saw a flicker of uncertainty on her face, and he smiled grimly. "What's the matter, have you forgotten what your lines were?"

"I *was* asleep," she said, "I don't know what I said."

"Almost, Eleanor," he said. "You almost had me going again. I don't know why you're pulling this number now, except maybe you're really afraid I might shoot you and you're trying to throw me off the track. But it won't work."

"But it's true," she pleaded. "Why don't you believe me?"

"Because Alec suggested I bring a gun here, and as peculiar as he is, he wouldn't have risked that there'd be an accident. I don't think he'd take a chance like that for an acting exercise."

"The gun won't go off," she said.

He glanced down at the weapon but saw nothing odd about it. "Alec emptied the powder out of the bullets," Eleanor continued.

Larry looked back up at her. "You're lying," he said.

In response, Eleanor let her raised leg fall to one side, totally exposing herself. She raised her arms and spread them across the pillows on either side of her. She presented a picture of complete vulnerability and openness, and an unmistakable invitation to sex. Larry tried to fight it, but his arousal grew stronger, and he felt the beginnings of an erection.

"You're the only man in my life," she said. "I knew I was losing you and I fought back the only way I knew how. You were using zen as a defense so I used acting as a weapon."

"And what's this place, your armory?"

"This house belongs to a friend of Alec's, a producer. You can check on that later if you like, but now I want something from you."

"What?"

"A decision. Either you want me as your woman or not. Make up your mind." She looked at him imploringly. "And listen to your heart."

Larry was transfixed. There was no room left in which to maneuver. His practice had pushed him against a wall and his wife had set the wall on fire. If he believed her now and she was lying, he'd never be able to trust his judgment again. If she was telling the truth and he didn't believe her, he'd lose her and his self respect. The sun had now hit its stride and was hot on his back.

Eleanor leaned toward him. "Larry," she said, "It's me." And she smiled.

But something in the expression caught at him. He gazed at her with wonder, recognizing a look that has haunted countless millions for centuries. It was the most famous smile in the world, that of La Giaconda, the Mona Lisa.

Then, as he was drawn more deeply into it, the expression changed. Eleanor's lips seemed to undergo a subtle transformation. They grew slightly more fleshy, more curved at the edges. This was more familiar in other cultures at other times, but Larry had seen it often enough on paintings and statues. It was the smile of the Buddha.

Larry swayed on his feet. He couldn't tell how much of what he saw was perception and how much hallucination. He felt ready to drop from exhaustion. "Is this *all* an illusion?" he thought, encompassing the whole of existence with his question.

"Are you all right?" Eleanor asked.

"I don't know what's real anymore."

"You can find out," she said, her voice floating on the morning air.

"How?"

"You can do one of three things. You can aim that thing at me and pull the trigger and know very fast whether I'm lying. Or you can put down the gun and walk out that door and never look back. Or you can come to bed and make love to me."

Larry stood unmoving, the three choices spinning in his mind. But even as he considered the enormity of his decision, Eleanor leaned forward and stretched, as casually as though she'd been reading a book and taken a break to yawn. It seemed, in the circumstances, the essence of callousness or carelessness, and Larry was aghast, until he saw that the gesture was studied, planned, the same kind of stilted acting she'd projected over the past week. Simultaneously, the movement raised her breasts and charged her skin with a tingle of voluptuousness that sent desire flushing through him. And in that instant, he knew.

Eleanor's stagey stretch became a real yawn, and she lay back against the pillows again. She looked very sleepy and gazed at him softly. Larry felt breath filling him. His mind was suddenly empty of all images and concerns. And his cock was hard, straining against his jeans.

The rest was simple. He lifted his arm, brought the gun to his temple, and pulled the trigger. And before he even heard the dull metallic click, he laughed, then spun around and hurled the weapon through the open window. He turned back to Eleanor.

"Want to play Scrabble?" he said, grinning, moving toward her, watching the light dance in her eyes.

KNIGHTSBRIDGE

presents gripping tales of

Suspense

___ **Burndown**   1-877961-06-X
Stuart Collins
An insane experiment by a brilliant scientist
has gone awry, bringing chaos to the com-
munity and the world to the brink of disaster.

___ **Fatal Choices**   1-877961-23-X
James Burke
A stunning thriller of murder and suspense
about a violent collision between high-
stakes radio and the sordid underworld of
drugs, prostitution, and organized crime.

___ **Keeper**   1-877961-37-X
Michael Garrett
He saved her, cared for her, and loved her.
He was her keeper and she was his prison-
er in this psychological thriller of possession
and self-delusion.

___ **Run for Your Life**   1-877961-03-5
Stuart Collins
She married a soldier and he married the
war. The marathon was their battlefield.

___ **The Hammer's Eye**   1-877961-72-8
R. A. Scotti
Powerbrokers and spymasters toy with the
lives of a Soviet sex spy and an American
SDI wizard in this international thriller.

Above titles $4.95 U.S. & Canada
See order form at back of book.

KNIGHTSBRIDGE

Order Form

In order to receive books by mail, please check the appropriate title, remove that page from its binding, and send it along with this order form to:

Knightsbridge Publishing
208 East 51st St.
New York, NY 10017

Please send me the book(s) I have checked on the included page(s). I am enclosing a total of $_____._____ (Please add $1.00 for one book and 50¢ for each additional book for shipping and handling.*) My check or money order made out to Knightsbridge Publishing is enclosed. (No cash or C.O.D.s please.)

Name: _____

Address: _____

Apt.: _____

City: _____

State (Prov.): _____

Zip (P.C.): _____

*NY residents add 8.25% sales tax, CA residents add 6.75%.